Lost In A Poet Storm

ALAN HINES

 www.trafford.com

North America & international
toll-free: 844-688-6899 (USA & Canada)
fax: 812 355 4082

BOOKS OF POETRY ALREADY PUBLISHED BY ALAN HINES,

1. Reflections of Love
2. Thug Poetry Volume 1
3. The Words I Spoke
4. Joyce
5. Constant Visions
6. Red Ink of Blood
7. Beauty of Love
8. Reflections of Love Volume 2
9. Reflections of Love Volume 3
10. True Love Poetry
11. Visionary.
12. Love Volume 1
13. This is Love
14. Garden of Love
15. Reflections of Love Volume 4
16. Reflections of Love Volume 5
17. Reflections of Love Volume 6
18. Reflections of Love Volume 7
19. Reflections of Love Volume 8
20. Reflections of Love Volume 9
21. Reflections of Love Volume 10

URBAN NOVEL ALREADY PUBLISHED BY ALAN HINES,

1. Book Writer
2. Queen of Queens

UPCOMING BOOKS OF POETRY BY ALAN HINES,

1. Reflections of Love Volume 3
2. This is Love (Volume 1, 2, and 3)
3. Founded Love (Volume 1, 2, and 3)
4. True Love (Volume 1, 2, and 3)

5. Love (Endless Volumes)
6. Tormented Tears (Volume 1, 2, and 3)
7. A Inner Soul That Cried (Volume 1, 2, and 3)
8. Visionary (Endless Volumes)
9. A Seed That Grew (Volume 1, 2, and, 3)
10. The Words I Spoke (Volume 2, and 3)
11. Scriptures (Volume 1, 2, and 3)
12. Revelations (volume 1, 2, and 3)
13. Destiny (Volume 1, 2, and 3)
14. Trials and Tribulations (Volume 1, 2, and 3)
15. 15. IMMORTALITY (Volume 1 ,2, and 3)
16. 16. My Low Spoken Words (Volume 1, 2, and 3)
17. Beauty Within (Volume 1, 2, and 3)
18. Red Ink of Blood (Volume 1, 2, and 3)
19. Destiny of Light (Jean Hines) (Volume 1, 2, and 3)
20. Deep Within (Volume 1, 2, and 3)
21. Literature (Volume 1, 2, and 3)
22. Silent Mind (Volume 1, 2, and 3)
23. Amor (Volume 1, 2, and 3)
24. Joyce (Volume 1, 2, and 3)
25. Lovely Joyce (Volume 1, 2, and 3)
26. Pink Lady (Volume 1, 2, and 3)
27. Mockingbird Lady (Volume 1, 2, and 3)
28. Godly tendicies (Volume 1, 2, and 3)
29. Enchanting Arrays (Volume 1, 2, and 3)
30. Harmony (Volume 1, 2, and 3)
31. Realism (Volume 1, 2, and 3)
32. Manifested Deep Thoughts (Volume 1, 2, and 3)
33. Poectic Lines of Scrimage (Volume 1, 2, and 3)
34. Garden of Love (Volume 1, 2, and 3)
35. Reflection In The Mirror. (Volume 1, 2, and 3)

UPCOMING NON-FICTION BOOKS BY ALAN HINES,

1. Time Versus Life
2. Timeless Jewels
3. The Essence of Time
4. Memoirs of My Life
5. In my Eyes To See
6. A Prisoner's Black History

UPCOMING URBAN NOVELS BY ALAN HINES,

1. Black Kings
2. Playerlistic
3. The Police
4. Scandalous Scandal
5. The West Side Rapist
6. Shattered Dreams
7. She Wrote Murder
8. Black Fonz
9. A Slow Form of Suicide
10. No Motherfucking Love
11. War Stories
12. Storm
13. Ghetto Heros
14. Boss Pimps
15. Adolescents
16. In The Hearts of Men
17. Story Teller
18. Kidnapping
19. Mob Ties

ACKNOWLEDGEMENTS

Heavenly Father thank you for blessing me to live to see another day; thank you for all your many blessings which include me writing and being able to publish another book.

CHAPTER 1

"**S**top hitting on me, Randell stop hitting on me," Thunder said as Randell continued slapping her around.....

Randell slapped her to the floor pulled down her jogging pants upped his dick, and started fucking her in the ass as she screamed, and yelled because of the tormenting pain.....

"Randell stop fucking me in my ass, stop fucking me in my ass, stop fucking me in my ass," she said in a screeching voice. As she continued to cry out, and plead for him to stop he didn't listen.....

Thunder screams awoke her daughter Neese up. Neese jumped out her bed ran to see what was going on with her mom. As she made it to the bedroom she seen her mom stretched out as Randell held her down slamming his dick off in her ass.

Randell nutted in her ass, and let her up. She jumped up crying.

"Aww naw you just fucked me in my ass, you fucked me in my ass, you fucked me in my ass," Thunder said.

Randell looked at his rock-hard dick. I wanna do it again, he thought to himself....

Thunder looked at her bedroom door, and seen Neese standing there....

"Neese, baby go to your room, and close the door," Thunder said.

Neese didn't move didn't want to leave her mom in distress....

"Neese, baby please go to your room everything is okay, I'll be there in a little while," Thunder said while whipping tears from her own eyes....

This time Neese listened. She walked back to her room laid in her bed, and put the cover over her head....

I hate that stud, Neese said to herself....

From that day forth Neese promised herself that she'd never let a man put his hands on her or disrespect her in any shape form or fashion....

Every time Neese would turn around Randell would violently domestically annihilate her mom....

In the back of Neese's young mind she wish the bitch Randell would literally die, and that her father was still living....

Although Neese's real father was killed when she was younger she'd still have constant pleasurable memories of him....

Neese's dad was a gang chief king of the Traveler ViceLords....

Each day after he was killed Neese would have these fond memories of all the long walks they'd have as her dad would talk her ears off implanting knowledge within her young mind so that in time she'd prevail to be a productive lady.....

"Sweetheart you must never eat pork, never poison your body with things that's no good for you," Will said. "Why daddy, why shouldn't I eat pork," Neese said to her father, in her mind as she reminisced to herself about her father. "In the Koran Allah father of the universe teaches us that his children are forbidden to eat Swine. The pig is one the most nastiest animal that exist. The pig consumes all types of nasty food to eat then those that eat the pig in turns will eat all the things the pig has ate. For those that eat pig will in turn find themselves in an early grave because of all the disease he has to offer to mankind." Will said....

"Sweetheart I know you're only a little girl, and I may talk you to death, but I'm giving you these timeless jewels to help you get through life. Life is what you make it and you're going to make the best out of your life," Will said....

"Once you get older and you start dating, you make sure the love and respect is mutual. Never let your boyfriend put his hands on you, the first time he put his hands on you, your relationship should be over," Will said.

"In life never sit back and wait on a Welfare check get up make moves. When and if you finish college that will be great, but my advice to you is to go to college so you can be your own boss, not working for someone's company and being called a boss. A lot of people got the word boss misunderstood; boss is when you are the owner or part owner a boss is not a supervisor or a manager. I know you're going to pick your own major when and if you do go to college, but consider studying law to be a lawyer. Lawyers are their own bosses, because they have their own law firm, and lawyers are respected even by the racist police, don't nobody want no trouble out of lawyers, not even politicians,; Will said.

As Will continued to hold his only child Nesse's hand walking her to school, as she looked up at her dad, and towards the sunlight as he kept talking to her about being productive in life, she didn't understand some of the things he was talking about, but listen attentively.....

CHAPTER 2

At an early age when Neese was only six years of age her dad was killed. Bullets ripped through his flesh separating life and death....

As years progressed along, she'd miss her dad more and more. Her dad was like her best friend, and a father mixed in one.

As the years continued to move on she would still have visions of her walking holding her dad's hand looking up at him, and up at the sun while he would feed her brain knowledge....

As a kid when it started to thunder and rain Neese would always run outside in the rain, she loved the rain. Sometimes after it rain, she would try to find a Rainbow to follow it so she could try to find the pot of gold after the Rainbow.

She loved the rain so much her mother nicknamed her Storm.

Although her dad was gone, and she was so young she'd still follow his guidelines. She maintained the best grades all through school. She'd get her class work done so fast that she would sit in class and write words down on a piece of paper. It started as thoughts and turned into rhymes which later turned into poetry.

A few times once she was done the teacher wondered what she wrote down, the teacher went over to read the paper come to find out it was poetry in which the teacher liked. Later the teacher had Storm to read one of her poems in front of the class; Storm thought the class would clown her, but contrary to her beliefs the class loved it....

All throughout grammar school Nesse stayed on the honor roll and in the gifted class....

Freshmen year in high school was a blast. She went to an all-girl school she noticed that the girls had always been jealous of her, so she stayed to herself. She maintained friends that didn't go to her school....

As years overlapped it was Storms senior year. The girls started spreading bogus rumors, about her being a lesbian and seeing her at a gay club and walking down the street holding hands with another woman, which wasn't true. Storm was a virgin would never even consider having sex with another woman, never even had sex with a man before. It went back to her youth as she'd look up to her dad, and the sun at the same time how he'd preach to her about being against homosexuality in which Storm was against. Storm investigated to see who was spreading bogus rumors. She found the girl who said it, and asked her if she said it, she said yes, she said it. Before Storm knew it, she had laid hands on her, and they was pulling each other hair and exchanging punches. The girl got the best of Storm, Storm pissed on herself. Days after the fight Storm was the talk of the town, she got her ass whopped and pissed on herself. Storm, and the girl she was fighting got suspended for a week. Storm never went back to embarrassed. She transferred to another school to finish the rest of the Senior year....

In time that small rumor of her being gay would haunt her mind for years to come....

After high school she took only on-line college courses. She wanted to study law like her father wanted her to but instead decided to take two different majors, math and computer science.

More, and more guys would be at her wanting to fuck, but she remained a virgin, she wasn't even willing to have a boyfriend until later on in the futuristic time of life.

She'd see her mom Thunder a crack head; it was like seeing the burning of eternal fire in the form of flesh. Throughout it all she always respected her mother no matter what, she loved her mom; she knew if her dad was still living her mom would've never turned into a drug addict. Her mom started getting high shortly after her dad was killed; to ease the pain of no longer having him there. In turns her mom met a deadbeat boyfriend that was a drug addict as well that use to punch her and beat her. As a kid Storm wished her mother's boyfriend would just die....

Storm lived in the hood she'd roam the streets sometimes as a way of being free. Each time she'd pass the dope spots in the hood the guys would always try to get with her, she always denied them she didn't want no street nigga. All the time she'd roam the streets in the hood she'd hear many of the guys putting issues on King Will constantly, to her that was so immature, and sounded like the repeating of a broken record.

Storm had heard about the poetry clubs but never been not even once but yearned for the day she could flex her skills on the open mic.

One day she visited the poetry club for an audition and to her surprise after the audition they told her she'd be hitting the open mic in a few days. The poem she recited at the audition was called my father's name: My father's name in vain so they glorify off fame.

> *Distribution for currency exchange hustling passing*
> *time*
> *as it's a game. By law we were supposed to uplift*
> *and safeguard our community enhance gain.*
> *Love life through the creators will to gain.*
> *The love the life the loyalty, in its entirety everything.*

The days that exchanged for moonlight nights in which a few of them passed and she was ready to hit the mic for the first time. She went backstage to meet the other poets, as smoke lingered in the room each poet was in their own zone, somewhere quiet in deep thought, while others was reciting poetry at a low tone....

Storm recognized this guy from her hood. His nickname and poet name were the same. He went by the nickname Tears. People gave him that name because as a kid his eyes use to shed tears for no giving reason. Later in life Tears felt that the tears he was shedding was because of the heartache and tears him, and other people would be shedding over the years....

Storm approached Tears....

"Hey man I never knew you did poetry," Storm told Tears. "I never knew you did poetry either," Tears told Storm....

Tears told Storm his story on how he went to jail served 15 years straight for a body and that's how he started writing poetry....

Tears caught a murder for the Vice Lord nation in return the nation showed no love a lesson learn. So tears had it in his mind that when he'd touch the streets again he'd never sell dope or do anything else to risk his freedom.

Tears would get paid a few hundred dollars every week from the poetry club. Tears didn't want to sell drugs or be humping at a factory so although he only made a few hundred a week it was still good for him....

All the poets got together for prayer.

Following prayer Tears was first on the mic. He recited a poem called: Flashback.

> *Flashbacks of mishaps lives that was confiscated wont be coming back, stuck in a institutionalized system and wont be getting back, no letters, no money orders to keep ones on track. Love that disappeared was never all that. Crisis those crying out to the Lord to get they life back, tougher laws but didn't stop or slow down the killings they just got even more hideous reckless off track. Visions of those stuck in a maze of undying cravings of controlled substances in which they'll have until death becomes, until they die. Blood stains of tears that flow freely from ones eyes seeing the ancient black lives inhumane like animals in time, sad to see black on black crime.*

Storm loved the poem it reminded her of something she would write herself. The second poet was named Lonnie Love, his real name was Lonnie, but he added the Love part to it because he writes mainly love poetry. Lonnie Love recited a poem called Nest:

> *My hatched love from Nest, love of lifetime.*
> *Mrs. Valentine.*
> *Holy Divine.*
> *Make love to my mind.*
> *My sunshine.*
> *My dream of love of life,*
> *within lifetime.*

Afterwards the audience stood up cheering and clapping....

The third poet was called Suicide. Just like all the other poets Suicide had a story to tell. Her story was that she was adopted as a child she never knew her real family and her adopted mother and father whom raised and loved her since she was a kid got killed in terrible car accident, she was left all alone is the cold world of frost circumstances. She named herself Suicide because she would constantly have thoughts of Suicide. Suicide first poem was called: Stained Mirror....

It was a stain in the mirror,
but yet and still she could see things clearer.
No Pilgrims or Happy Thanksgiving,
but instead roaches that fell from ceilings.
Gun shots of killings.
Abandon building living.
Mice that walked around as if they rented.
Kris Kringle ponded gifts on Christmas.
She'd bare witness to those that got high
as the only way to achieve a wonderful prism.
Over packed prisons of those that didn't listen
didn't abide by the fundamental written
guidance of the literature.
She'd seen those before her that made wrong
decisions, she'd let that be a lesson learned
off others failed missions.
Those that's telling the ones secretly planted
kisses.
Obituaries of those we love R.I.P. we miss them.
Lives that was confiscated over foolish and
petty issues.
She blanked out and broke all mirrors, more
then seven years bad luck superstition would
definitely continue.
Took a piece of the broken mirror and slide
both of her wrist tissue,
couldn't live the life of reality of a stain
mirror.

It was Storm's first time on the mic, she was nervous. Suicide gave her a pep talk told her to not to be scared but instead try to imagine if they wasn't there as if she was home alone.

Storm stepped to the mic scared to death she tried to use the method that Suicide told her, but it didn't work. Storm had a poem memorized but couldn't get it out so she just freestyled: Lady liberty.

> *Lady light.*
> *Free us from bondages of life.*
> *Give us new life.*
> *Never ignorant getting goals accomplished, in life.*
> *Paradise.*
> *Delight.*
> *The things I like.*
> *The soothing words of poetry I write.*
> *The breezing through times,*
> *the days of our lives.*
>
> *Lady liberty.*
> *Lady light.*
> *Give us a sign of the time*
> *a visionary of sight.*
>
> *Lady liberty.*
> *Lady light.*

Everyone liked Storms poetry, her poetry was deep....

After the poetry club was over that night Storm went home and seen her mom eyes wide open foaming at the mouth, as if she had become part of the lifeless. Storm panicked and ran over to her shaking her saying her name back to back.

"I'm good stomach aching," Storm's mom Thunder said.

Storm looked at her mom's head seen it was nappy, looked at the thinness of her body brought back memories of when her mom was young and beautiful when her dad was still living before the drugs conquered her mom's existence. Storm could slightly smell the aroma of her mom's pussy, and knew she'd been out selling pussy. Storm loved her mom to death but hated seeing her mom as a drug fiend....

Once Suicide made it home in which she lived all alone, once again she wanted to commit Suicide. She looked at the window and just wanted to jump head first. She went into the bathroom looking in a stained mirror just like in her poem. While looking in the mirror in a split second she admired her own beauty while still living, as she could see herself lying dead inside a casket. With no second guess she grabbed a bottle of pills and took all 18 of them. Within moments of time she passed out on the bathroom floor. To only wake up the next day still living, such a disappointment for her....

The poetry club was only open three days a week Thursday, Friday, Saturday. Storm made a showing to recite pieces of poetry each time it was open. She began to question the owner of the club about why she wasn't getting paid when the other poets was getting paid. The owner told her it goes off request, once the audience start requesting her she would start getting paid....

Once weeks passed along the audience begin to request Storm more and more, started getting paid. Her pay was only several hundred a week, which was good for her because she lived with her family, Storm quit her job at the Supermarket and just survived off the money she was making from the poetry club.

Coincidently one night while at the club it rained outside. Tears would look out the window drowning in sorrow wishing for a better day tomorrow. Storm went over to talk to Tears, come to find out they had one thing main thing in common they both love the rain. Ever since he was a kid Tears always believe that when it rained that God was crying tears, that the raindrops were God's teardrops, because of the madness and sins his children would commit non-stop. Storm told Tears that she loved the rain, she even loved going out and getting wet in the rain, she told Tears that's how she got her name Storm....

At all times when Storm would hear gun shots, she lived in the hood so it was so common to her, but she despised that the gun shots came from Travelers against Travelers, the Travelers off the Double Up, was waring with the Travelers off Albany. Storm knew if her dad was still living there was no way ViceLords would be waring with one another, especially the Travelers that was her dad's very own branch of ViceLord....

CHAPTER 3

"**G**ive a round of applause for poet Suicide," The announcer at the club said, as Suicide got on the mic, and blanked out reciting her poem she wrote titled Mental Disaster: Mental pics of my own self lying dead in a casket. killed by a teenager that had no father, no parental guidance, he was a dirty bastard.

Mental Pics of me being a slave, and having to call another human being master, what a disaster.

Mental pics of me being in the midst of the dragon, the beast empire doing sinful works being yelled at to do it faster.

Mental pics of me being stuck in a mental institution, seeing illusions, confusions.

A prison of disaster, everlasting.

Souls that shall get eternal life in hell, burn in eternal fire.

Drugs that took people higher.

A socialism of Pinocchio's liars and evilness of preaching pastors....

Mental images of disaster.

Next to the mic was Tears, Tears recited a poem:

*Caught in a whirlwind bloody teary eyes of maze.
Kidnapping our
black sisters same as ancient African slave trades.
Land of Sodom
and Gomorrah rainbow parades, newborns born with
H.I.V. virus
around the time they reach an adolescent full blown
A.I.D.S.
In Jesus name I pray for better days. Those wrongfully
convicted
natural life on bunks in cells they shall lay. Teenagers
straight
killers that will take your life away. Bloody holidays.
This
is the land the lives God made; Lucifer sick self
leading the troops astray....*

Next to the mic was Father Time:

*Time could never rewind. If only we had the powers
to turn back the hands of time. Give a sight, a vision
to the blind, leading the blind. Live righteously, holy
and divine. Great things seek and find. Get through
troublesome times. Prepare right now for in the future
we shall overcome, we shall shine. In due time what
was in the dark shall come to light to shine, we shall
overcome we shall be considered divine.*

Next to the mic was Sight:

*I've seen those living breathing to those in caskets
dead. Joy and happiness, days of stress upon head.
Seen those free, and those confined away, calendars*

to shred. Seen those that was rich, same ones poor,
and mislead. Seen those that was thought to be good
but was snakes instead. Seen my only love I ever had
turned out to be a lesbian in bed......

CHAPTER 4

"Mom want you stop drinking the doctors been told you that you won't live long if you keep drinking," Tears told his mom. "Fuck you, who is you to tell me stop drinking I don't say nothing we ya'll smoke ya'll weed and pop pills all day," Tears mom said. "But me smoking weed ain't life threatening," Tears said....

Tears went back and forth arguing with his mom about how she should stop drinking. She had just left the hospital body failure from drinking, she went straight from the hospital to the liquor store....

The doctor had told her years ago that if she keeps drinking she wont live very long.....

It was hard for her to stop drinking, liquor was her life, and would mentally take her away from this cold world we lived in.

Tears loved his mom dearly. Tears would remember the times when he was locked up trapped in a time frame stuck in the belly of the beast, where love from the homies the nation of ViceLord was deceased. His mom was his only love, only peace.

If he didn't have his mom there would've been no money, no visits, no letters of love in existence. Over time everybody broke bad on him even his own family which was sad....

When times when he was feeling mental distortion, he'd go talk to his auntie Louise. Louise was an ex crack head that stop getting high and gave her life to the Lord.

When Louise did get high, she'd drift to a world of reality as it seems she speak her mind as a black queen. A lot of people didn't like being around her when she was high because they say she'd talk too much. But Tears loved it because she'd speak the truth.

When Louise did get high sometimes, she'd like to smoke in the closet. The first time Tears caught Louise smoking in the closet, he just yelled out, "you a closet smoker," as they both begin laughing.

Previous in life when Louise would take a blast of the missile filled with rock cocaine, as she'd speak her mind as it remains.

She'd take her mouth of the missile and began; "what the Italians did in the past black people doing in today but just on a different level of drug dealing they were more organized than blacks. No matter how laws change, people, places and things change drug dealings will never stop because people gone always get high," Louise said.

She'd take another hit off the missile inhaling, and exhaling the smoke; "I heard your cousin caught a drug case, I had a case one time just shopping for a few bags and the police caught me right after I purchased the bags. It was chaotic I couldn't speak up to defend myself everybody including my public defender was white, you just sit back and roll with the flow, they should at least allow you to say a little something to defend yourself but they don't, for all they know the police could've planted those drugs on me," Louise said.....

Tears snapped back to his current day and age as he ceased to contemplate of Louise former life when she was an addicted.

Tears begin to talk to Louise about his mom's drinking problem, that would someday make her fatal if she didn't stop. Louise told him is nothing he could do but leave it in God's hand and continue to pray....

The next night in the poetry club Tears was first on the mic:

"A never ending saga consumptions of alcohol and drug usage as a way of feeling a wonderful prism, from life from a distance problems, non-existence. Some will even pond the kids gift at Christmas. Please stop drinking. Love life to be increasing. We need you down here on Earth as an angelic creature."

The next poet to the mic was Lonnie Love:

"She open my eyes to the sight of her rise. I'd visualize family ties, mom's apple pie, Heaven in the sky, babies that will never even cry. Legitimate reasoning why. An angel descending on Earth in my eyes. No surprise, flawless images of her in my eyes. No foolish pride. No games being utilize.

She opened my eyes to love that seem to be cast from the skies. Gave me sight as I was once blind. A love affair that I could never find. Intellect of a female version of Albert Einstein.

She opened my eyes to what the creator had design; what I was put on Earth to mastermind; to be all I can be and shine until the end of time.

She opened my eyes to the true love in her heart that was enshrined.

She opened my eyes to this love for her kind.

She opened my eyes.

The next poet was Suicide:

Drowning in time.
Drowning in my own blood.
The completion of lifelines.
No happy Valentine's.
This little light of mine I'm gonna let
it shine.
Blind leading blind.
Civilizations decline.
This is your brain on drugs
as the eggs continue frying.

Once Suicide left the club, she had constant visions of Suicide as usual. Once she made it home, she stared in the stained mirror in her bathroom wishing she could die.

She grabbed a razor contemplated on sliding her risk but didn't want to feel such pain. She sat the razor down and went looking out her project window, wanted to take to the sky and fly before she'd die, but didn't have the courage....

CHAPTER 5

One night as Storm entered the back of the club as usual, she came in contact with the midst of smoke as all the poets were in the own zone. Some would be recited poetry to themselves at a low tone, others would be writing down poetry, while others would simply be brain storming.

Storm stepped to Tears as they begin a deep and meaningful conversation. While talking to Tears Storm noticed it was a few new poets; in the back of her mind she couldn't wait to her them rock the mic, Storm was hungry to hear poetry, craving as an appetite as a since of delight, sky rockets in flight.....

While talking to Tears she noticed this guy from her hood named Lil Wayne. She had always had a secret crush on him when she was a kid, but he was too old for her, he was about ten years older than her.

She stepped away from Tears and went to talk to Lil Wayne, she thought he didn't remember her, but he remembered her very well, although he hadn't seen her since she was a little girl.

At this point in time although he was ten years older than her it didn't matter because they were both adults.

Storm came to find out just as Tears Lil Wayne started writing poetry while he was in the joint. Lil Wayne poetry name was Sidney; he gave himself that nickname because as he'd felt like when he recited his poetry he wanted to act out like Sidney Poitier.

Lil Wayne was a player he could talk ho's into doing the things for him that they wouldn't normally do for other guys. As she'd conversate with him freely of things in life as a visionary to see, the blossoming of eternal seeds of eternity, she felt free as can be. As Lil Wayne laid his mac down, she'd look into his low red eyes as he was high off smoking loud as a free enterprise. She began rubbing on his back as he'd spit game like a ancient pimp that had his eyes on the prize....

Eventually Lil Wayne, and Storm begin hanging out. Lil Wayne treated her like a queen. Storm was shocked that Lil Wayne never tried to have sex with her. What she didn't know that Lil Wayne would never try to have sex with her, he would just continue to mess around with her until she was ready, he knew she was a virgin and if he ever got the pussy he would have her on lock.

Lil Wayne would spend lots of money on her, take her places she never been before. Lil Wayne even hooked her up to do some shows here and there with some of the underground rappers he knew; she was even featured reciting poetry on a few of their songs, which was good all the way around the board, quick ways to make some extra cash.

After many months of Storm, and Lil Wayne being together he didn't even have to ask Storm wanted to give him the pussy. Her virgin body was calling for him to serve and protect it.

As their tongues tasted the sweetness of each others mouth, as they embarked into erotica. He swiftly took off her shirt and bra sucking the titties as if he was breast feeding. Pants and panties to the floor as his mouth connected to her pearl tongue, she was sprung. He turned around and ate her ass to her it was such a dynamic blast.

Now it was time for the moment of truth as he Vaseline his dick down it took him some time to enter, but once he did the hollering and scratches on his back overlapped....

He wanted to taste her Vagina lips once again, he wanted to taste her soul as pleasure would come to be as pleasures would unfold....

CHAPTER 6

More and more the family cried out to Tears mom to stop the drinking, but she loved alcoholic beverages as it seemed alcohol made her feel supreme.

He'd have visions of when he was in prison, and his mom was there when no one else was. He wrote a poem about it:

> *as I rotted away in jail cells, time shall reveal time*
> *shall prevail. Freedom or jail, Heaven or Hell.*
> *Defecation*
> *as a permanent smell, I need commissary, I need*
> *letters*
> *I need mail. All as well. Thou shall never fail.*
> *Against*
> *the system I rebel. Phonies, I still love you and wish*
> *you well.*

Tears went to talk to his auntie Louise again, and she told him again to put it in God's hand and that it's not easy for people to stop drinking, using drugs, or smoking Cigarettes, life was hard and those things would ease the pain of living, God bless the child, God bless his children.

To the naked eye Tears seem like a peaceful smooth dude, but at all times internally he was as a maniac, his mind was that of being locked in a cage amongst other maniacs going insane, loss of hope, loss of brain. Tears would have constant visions of being sprayed in the face with mace, and officers hollering in his face, begging to God that he don't catch a new case.

Tears often cried out to God to take away his pain, but his pain remained.

Tears smoked loud and ate Edibles to ease the pain.

His cousin Todie introduced him to eating Edibles. Edibles was candy gummy bears with weed cooked in them. Edibles was the best drug Tears ever felt it took his mind and body into a world of matrix. The only problem was that Todie's connect on the Edibles didn't have them all the time, and they didn't know anybody else that supplied them in need in demand.

As another white cop killed another innocent black man caught on tape. The police didn't even want to charge the cop at first. The Blacks across the United States of America rocked the streets; it was no race war as previous decades ago, but uncontrollably looting all throughout days and nights, blacks against the police even some fist fights, in several cities burning down police stations, God bless your children God please help the nation.

Tears never got involved in any looting, fighting the police, or protest. He prayed to God for the best....

Tears would be high in a zone, spilling his guts in his poetry: History repeats water hose and dogs on human beings we are we. My country tears I see, no sweet lady of liberty. High as the whistling skies, as a new day begun, we need more guns, we need more troops. Living in a land where my great grandfather was slave and died. Raped our women as they cried. Let us come together to be victory as one to coincide....

Roaming the streets, the looting of burning fire, souls of the lake eternal fire. Drugs taking higher. Madness, death, destruction, the sick ones admired. Traded in the sheets, a badge and uniform are their new entire. In reality we will never be equal a part of their empire. Expiration date of lives soon to expire. Taking higher.

Tears poem noise:

> *The noise, I can't stand the noise rapid gunfire stray*
> *bullets hit the babies as they play in*
> *playgrounds with their toys. Little boys, sleeping with*
> *other little boys. Can't even sleep they*
> *on the gallery screaming and hollering about nonsense*
> *the poison in which boils, driving me*
> *crazy with all that noise.*

CHAPTER 7

S uicide went around the corner from where she lived and paid 30 dollars for a dipped Cigarette, dipped in PCP water. She went home staring in her stained mirror fired up her dip Cigarette as things became clearer.

While still smoking the dip Cigarette she begins to look out her project window. In her own silent mind, she wanted to fly soar like a bald eagle, so high. How high. She wanted to reach the sky. She really believed she could fly, she literally wanted to touch the sky one day before she die. She sat by looking out her project window smoking the last of the dip Cigarette to get high with no hesitation she jumped out of the window saying, "I can fly, I can fly, I can fly," right before her skull hit the ground cracking open many times. She wanted to fly a suicidal way to die. Could never be forgiving for that suicidal sin she had to try, no Heaven in the sky. Her soul shall forever burn in eternal fire. Right before she died, she wanted to fly.

Once all the poets found out everyone was devastated. They couldn't believe that she committed suicide, but it was the truth.

She was so young never had a chance to grow, never grew, never knew.

Suicide had no family so the owner of the poetry club decided to pay for the funeral. Although she had no family the funeral was pack; silent tears will forever shed throughout years. They did not bury her, the owner of the poetry club had heard from two different people that she wanted to be cremated, and she wanted her cremated ashes to blow away in the skies.

Coincidently the day of Suicide's cremation was on a windy day. As the crowds stood with lit candles they opened the container poured out her cremated ashes as it became magical, like a magic show as her cremated ashes blew away in the skies....

A week later Storm mom Thunder died; her cause of death was an overdose on Heroin. For years Thunder just smoked rocked cocaine, but graduated to treating her nose with dope, which caused her death....

Storm would be shock up for the rest of her natural life; at the funeral her tears drowned her face as if someone had threw a bucket of water on it. Storm's mom and dad was gone her life would never be the same. But Storm made a solemn promise to herself to keep striving for excellence, continue with her on-line classes and graduate, and maintain....

Two weeks after Storm's mom died Tears was having on going episodes with his mom in and out the hospital every other day. Each time she'd leave the hospital she'd go right to the liquor store. Until one day at the hospital as doctors and nurses battled to save her life, her life came to an end. As Tears stood outside the hospital room, within time all the doctors and nurses left the room without saying a word. Tears knew what time it was. Tears entered the room Todie, and the rest of the family came shortly after as Tears entered the room, he stepped towards his mom's hospital bed and seen his mom eyes wide open blood shot red eyes as streaks of blood leaked from mouth and eyes.

his cousin Todie begin screaming to cry, cries that shall last to the ending of time.

He sat and watch the tube in her mouth bubbling blood.

To doctors and nurses it was just a job, to him and his family the love of life had been robbed.

Tormented and torn he'd forever mourn.

His inner soul of everlasting tears would haunt him as a nightmare for the rest of years he'd live.

He'd effortlessly, endlessly pray that upon judgment day the Heavenly Father would uplift her soul for eternal life above the clouds she'd forever stay. It'll never in life be nothing no one could do or say to whip his tears away.... The sight of his mom laid in the bed dead would haunt him for the rest of his natural life.....

Nobody wanted to help him with the funeral cost, although many of his family members had lots of money, to them money wasn't a thing. They just didn't want to help. Tears got more love from strangers that didn't even know his mom, sad. Alot of his mom's siblings didn't even come to the funeral nor didn't even help pay for it, those that did help pay only put up crumbs....

After the funeral throughout life Tears disowned certain family members because they showed him how fake they really was....

CHAPTER 8

Tears stayed in deep thoughts. He'd think about everything that was going on as far as the past present and the future. Tears would watch the news and as usual another innocent black man was killed by the police, or either brutally beaten by the police.

The police killed a black man on tape for the hundredth time, it seemed as Tears was losing his mind. Troublesome time, the white officers was killing blacks, and it was an increase on black on black crime, if only Tears could stop the blood clot crying.

Tears would compare prison to slavery. The prison system would consist of majority white officers and white staff members, but majority of the inmates were blacks. To the whites it was just a job. But in reality, it was modern day slavery they controlled the movement of the inmates they used them as industry workers in prison paid them crumbs to produce goods for companies in the free world to make themselves more money. To Tears their past history hangings was when the police in the free world would innocently kill Blacks, or give blacks the death penalty, in a court of law.

When the violence slowed down Tears would roam the streets at night and see how the structure of ViceLord just wasn't the same. Most of the young ViceLords didn't even know their literature or the concept of founded foundation of ViceLord. It would be constant gun fire ViceLord against Vicelord going against the law of Vicelord.

Tears often wonder to himself was we living in our last days a sick land filled with gay parades, violence madness dismay, he'd often pray for better days.

Most nights Tears couldn't sleep visions of so many things would haunt his sleep. All the times he'd have nightmares of his mom in the hospital bed dead as streaks of blood ran down her face. Sometimes in his sleep he'd hear gun shots from project building to building senseless killings. Nightmares of Militia men killing African children....

Tears would have nightmares as if he was still in prison, no commissary, no love within existence.

One night Tears had a dream he was drowning. In the dream he was an African kidnapped from Africa and put on slave ship as they sailed down the middle passage the load on the boat was to heavy the whites threw some of the Africans in the water the drown to die; in his dream he was one of the Africans thrown in in the water of unchangeable tides to longer live to die, eternal tears to cry.

Caught by surprise as Tears turned to the CNN news a white cop killed a 7 year-old black girl shot twice with a .45 automatic one in the face the other ripped through her chest instantly separating life and death Heavenly father please assist within itself......

The father of the seven year old girl that got killed was devastated mind clouded with the sin hate, his only seed life was robbed, stolen, and took away.

The father of the seven year old was a security guard whom was on the verge of being a regular city cop but after his daughter was heinously murdered, he knew he could never become a police part of the unjust, unGodly system.

Years later as the trial became the officer was found not guilty for shooting the little girl twice taking her life line from her....

As the officer exited the court building several news cameras surrounding him as the father of the slain seven year-old ran to his car ran back up to the police officer, and shot him twice in the brain, instantly putting the cop to death no longer breathing. As the cop body dropped the father of the seven year-old dropped his gun to the ground as he held his hands in the air awaiting for the police to come arrest him.....

At the trial of the father of the seven year-old girl he was sentenced to spend the rest of his Natural Life in prison....

As years overlapped the father of the slain seven year-old felt zero regrets for killing the cop and having to spend the rest of his life in prison; his only dilemma was that he would have to live the rest of his life without his daughter....

CHAPTER 9

With so much death and destruction going on in this cold world the poets at the club begin to pour out their hearts more within their poetry. The owner of the club made Storm the manager of the poetry he felt she was the best one fit for the position....

One night Storm showed up a little late to the club she entered and as usual through the back once she entered as always she noticed clouds of smoke everyone sipping liquor from the bar out of large glasses. She noticed that the environment seemed as if it was tension in the air. There was no tension in the air all the poets were just feeling some type of way and eager to pour out their hearts on the mic, allowing their poetry to be as a fire to ignite.

Storm called all the poets together for prayer before they started their performance: "Heavenly Father whom are in Heaven thank you for blessing us to live to see another day, allow your eternal love to forever more shine our way. Please continue to look over our family members and friends, please guide us and protect us with no end. Allow us as poets to be prosperous and poetry to be felt as a must. In Jesus name we pray, Amen," Storm said as all the poets said Amen as well.

The first poet to the mic was Lonnie Love:

> *"In her eyes you could see the sunrise. Living on Earth as it is in Heaven before the last days of demise. Happily, ever after marriages, the beginning of family ties. Living forever no funerals to cry. Her love was like a blessing from the creator up and beyond the skies. In her eyes I could see babies being born, teaching the kids shoelaces to tie, as they grow to teenagers teaching them how to drive. She was and still such a lovely lady seeing the burning love in her eyes, dignity and pride. What was her's was mines. A love that was blessed and cast from beyond the skies. I could literally see Angels in her eyes. This love of mines paradise in her eyes."*

The next poet was a female named Life, reciting a poem called The City of Abundant life:

> *"She was from the city of Abundant Life. Prayed to God through Jesus Christ. Sanctified is the way she chose to live life. A virgin like Mary, Joseph's wife. She made others take flight. High off scriptures, and life. Fun-loving, and nice. For each offering she gave twice. Didn't care of other downfalls, or sick sinful delights; she'd still preach to them about Christ. She said once she die, she'd wanted to be buried in the city of Abundant life."*

The third poet was Tears:

"Another teenager was killed, dismay wish he could live again, whip your tears, tears away, tears away. Live to see another day. Live life free as the stars, the sun shines your way."
Grow, grow old as your bearded hair turns gray. Spread your wings like a bald Eagle loving as a sequel, we shall overcome but never be equal. Live your life young man and be a person for the people."

The fourth poet was Sidney:

"Reality formed. Once upon a time in America there were artwork, poetic love poems.
Little girls getting their dreams to have Ponies and Unicorns until reality came
in the form of a storm.
Barking dogs' sirens and the sounds of burglar alarms.
Killed their own parents, children of the corn.
Behold of the pale white horse with a horn like a unicorn.
Hurricanes, floods, and thunderstorms.
Blood dripping and pouring.
Continuous deaths, and mourning.
Tormented racist legislative candidates in closets performing.
The last days of Revelation is up and forming....
Reality in its rawest form."

CHAPTER 10

Tears and Storm begin hanging out together, nothing outta the ordinary but just as friends. The first time they went out they went to the gun range; it was Storm's first time holding and shooting a gun she'd like the power it would bring made her feel supreme like a queen. The gun range was love for Tears and Storm because so much sin was being committed down here on Earth, the shootings the killings the racism the unjust Judicial system that it was a form a way for them to momentarily relieve stress and for to be momentarily free from burdens of life.

Over time Sidney begin to suspect that Tears and Storm was fucking but reality they weren't they were more like brother and sister.

Sidney started to hang out with Tears and Storm, afraid what could happen if he wasn't around.

One night Sidney told Storm how he felt about her and Tears hanging out. "Never will I cheat on you, you are the only one for me," Storm said.

As Sidney was laid on the bed Storm got on her knees with an aim to please, she pulled his dick out looked at it as she was examining it and started pleasuring his dick with her mouth as she'd commence to licking it like a female dog, and then sucking it.....

Together Storm and Tears would go out to help those in centers of rehabs, wanting those to be sober freely as an aftermath.

They'd go out with attempts to feed the homeless on the streets to the best of their ability by neither one of them having large sums of money.

They'd visit shelters providing clothes from the Goodwill, and food, and information on jobs that was hiring.

Overtime Tears begin to teach Storm ViceLord literature and the concepts of ViceLord. Storm love hearing and learning ViceLord literature because it was deep....

CHAPTER 11

T ears started taking more drugs to ease the pain of living. He smoked Loud, popped pills, and eat Edibles. The more he'd be high his sex drive would increase....

Tears got a new apartment outside the hood, and it was this cute white chick that lived in the same building as Tears she was nineteen, Tears was almost forty. Tears didn't believe in having sex with girls that young but he had seen her one day in some skimpy shorts in which sparked up a sexual interest.

One day Tears decided to strike up a conversation. Come to find out her name was Becky. Becky had been liking Tears and had did her homework on Tears.

As Tears begin talking to Becky, she told him that she heard he write poetry and that she would be interesting in hearing some of it.

Tears invited Becky to his house to read her some poetry. Together they smoked loud and in no time, Tears was talking her outta her clothes, shoes, and socks.

Tears seen her cute little shaved white pussy and immediately stated eating her shit. This was her first time getting her pussy ate, she'd never gave oral sex, or received it to her this was wonderful felt like paradise. As Tears continued licking her Pearl Tongue it felt so good it felt like she was getting ready to cry.

Tears put his dick in her little tight pussy in no time the juices and berries begin flowing. Tears begin giving her the dick as she moaned, he started to kiss her in the mouth while still feeding her pussy the dick. In no time he was slamming his dick in and out her pussy harder as the nut exploded in her he held his dick in her without moving it for a minute......

By her living in the same building they would have sex on a frequent level.

Eventually Tears convinced Becky to start sucking his dick, she'd even swallow the nut. Becky would like to get on her knees to suck his dick as he'd read to her poetry....

Becky had wanted to do a threesome with Tears, with her Mexican female friend from work. Tears couldn't believe that Becky asked him for a threesome....

Once they did do the threesome Becky, and her Mexican friend was more happy than Tears. They came in Tears house not saying a word and immediately got undressed. Tears begin kissing both girls in the mouth one by one as he himself undressed. Once he undressed the girls remained on their feet as Tears felt to his knees eating the Mexican Pussy first while he fingered Becky. And then he switched up he ate Becky pussy while fingering the Mexican....

Becky sat on the Mexican's face as Tears fed the Mexican his dick hardcore....

As Tears bust a nut in the Mexican's pussy he stood up took his dick out her pussy put it in Becky's mouth as she started sucking his dick, the Mexican started eating his balls, therefore he was getting his dick and balls ate at the same time.

Tears fucked the Mexican damaged the pussy. Then he fucked Becky as she moaned in the midst of pleasure and pain the Mexican just watched in pleasure. The girls then took turns fucking each other with a Dildo strap on. Then from the back Tears fucked them one by one while each ate the other one's pussy.... After the threesome Tears and Becky became real close....

CHAPTER 12

Storm wanted to try Edibles she heard they were a bomb. Tears tried his best to convince her not to....

Storm ending up getting the Edibles from Sidney. Sidney was more than glad to give her Edibles. Sidney loved for his girlfriends to get high, because the sex was great when both partners are high....

Storm first time eating the Edibles she went into a world of matrix. She felt as if she walking upon the clouds, as she began to spit poetry out loud. The Edibles had her feeling the best feeling she ever felt in life.....

Days to follow she begin to smoke loud, pop pills, and sip a little Champagne in which amplified her high off the Edibles.

Being high made her feel like queen of the world; a periodic paradise, love but twice as nice, as Sidney would be the love of her life.....

The more she got high the more she wanted hardcore sex. She begin to spend more time at Sidney's house as all the while there, she'd walk around in the nude. As Sidney loved every moment of it.....

"Come over here and suck this dick," Sidney told Storm as she obeyed his order.

Storm walked over to Sidney as he was laid on the bed, she got on her knees with a aim to please she pulled down his boxers as she let the saliva build up in her mouth as she placed it on his dick and started sucking it being nasty with it she used one of her hands to jag him off as she continued sucking the dick.....

Sidney never understood why Storm like sucking dick so much. What Storm never told him was that she liked sucking dick so much because it made her cum better than when he was fucking her......

After she finished sucking it she got on top placed his dick in her pussy and took him on a rodeo show.....

After nutting in the pussy she sucked it for a little while just so it could get back hard. Once it got hard right on the kitchen floor she got on all fours as he gently placed his dick in her pussy and commenced to beating the the pussy up from the back, as he would talk dirty to her and slap her ass cheeks all at the same time.....

Storm felt as her life was a love story from a romance novel that came to life. To her Sidney was the love of life wonderful a delight. Will and might. She'd yearn to be with him throughout the rest of the days of her life.....

As she'd be high off loud and Edibles Sidney would eat her pussy and finger her as well taking her to an all new ultimate high of pleasure; from the initial time she got high and had sex she never wanted to be sober and have sex again she had to be high to the sky as sexual relations would rely.

To Storm having Sidney was a dream come true.....

CHAPTER 13

A s Storm entered the back stage of the poetry club she noticed as usual it was filled with clouds of smoke as some had glasses filled with liquor some had brown, while others had clear.....

It was so much chaos and madness in the world that the poets all could feel pain and they were as growling pit bulls ready to unleash their anger, but only in the form of poetry.....

"Everybody come together for prayer," Storm said.....

As everyday sat down their drinks and put out whatever they were smoking, quick, fast, and in a hurry everybody made their way to the center for prayer.....

"Heavenly Father thank you for blessing us to still be here living. Thank you for blessing us to be your children, the love, the support, the guidance, and healing. Thank you for loving us regardless, thank you God for being marvelous, in Jesus name I pray, Amen," Storm said as everybody else said amen all at once.....

First to the mic was Sidney:

"*Growed up. I growed up in the days of old, silently staring in the mirror reminiscing of my youth turned cold. By dope fiends, pipe smokers it was stole, and sold for the low. Visions of me looking out of my project windows and seeing mom, and dad when they were young before substances took control. Visions of my own kids leading themselves astray, away from the prism of what the creator unfold. Lucifer's powerful hold control lost souls those seeking fortune and fame, and the glitter, and gold. Since the days of old I grew up, I growed.*"

The second poet to the mic was Tears:

"*Paradox. A paradox of raging bulls that spit. On pulpits preachers sit scheming on ways to get rich. Sick sexual cravings that's obviously evident. Those that prey on those without street sense, common sense, tricking off money spent, young ladies that turn out to do whatever they are sent.*
A paradox of nasty dirty old man looking for flesh of teenage kids. Watching for the police as crimes they commit.
Throwing bricks at the pin begging for a way in. Curse kids because of lives of Bastard parents sin. Many men shall burn within the heart of Devil's fire skin. This is the life we shall never change, never give in.
Murdering childhood friends, lil grammar school girls pregnant with twins by grown men. A positive test of H.I.V. as your life shall end. This is your brain on drugs, as real brain cells are frying. Witnessing testifying, grown men crying, the jail cells they shall

die in. Starvation and mayhem. Puddles of blood
newborns lie, and die in, continuous crying. Ladies
bodies perverts buying in this paradox of eternal life I
shall never die in..... A paradox of continuous crying."

CHAPTER 14

S torm would have fun with Sidney in abundance as they'll be high of more than life he'd take her soaring in paradise. Lovely as a delight.

Majority of the days you'd see Sidney you'd see Storm right by his side love and peace to coincide. Together they'd live, Storm prayed that they'd be together until they'd die.....

"Eat the pussy first," Storm said as Sidney obeyed. All the while, while Sidney was eating the pussy he couldn't wait to push his dick in the pussy. Once he was finished eating the pussy he laid her on her back and begin beating the pussy up, this particular time it seemed as if her pussy was as wet than any time before, pussy galore.

Not only did Sidney please her body but he also made love to her mind, the best love she felt she'd ever find, spiritually and divine.....

Storm had always suspected Sidney of cheating but never got caught in the act, so she never brought it up.....

Normally she'd call Sidney to come pick her up when she wanted to be with him which was almost every day. This particular day she had got a rental car because she had lots a business to attend to and didn't want to be a burden on him so she decided to just surprise him. As Storm pulled up his block she seen a man and woman kissing as if the were in love with each other as no one existed but them. As she pulled closer she thought to herself, that look like Sidney. As she got closer she noticed it was Sidney kissing another woman. As a tear slid down her left cheek she whip the tear away and got out and confronted him in a peaceful civilized manner. Sidney blanked out and put hands on Storm busting her nose and giving her a black eye. Storm couldn't believe he'd do that especially after she got out the car talking in a civilized manner. She took off to her car and got in it speeding away. Her first mind was to go to the police station, but she changed her mind and went home cleaned up the blood stains, and got high to ease the pain.....

Days later Storm gave Sidney a call, he apologized for his actions she told him that she missed him and wanted to see him, and that she was on her way to him.

Sidney offered to come pick her up but she said no because it was raining outside and she wanted to enjoy walking in the rain.....

As she entered his home she tongued kissed him as if she was actually French, French kissing. Storm undressed out of her soaking wet rainy clothes, as they'd gaze out the window visualizing the crescent moon.....

As he ate her pussy she'd position herself to suck his dick at the same time as both received pleasure, both was giving pleasure.....

Once they started fucking Sidney beat the pussy up like never before as moaning, scratches on back, and the release of sperm, and cum became as one.....

As Sidney laid in a peaceful sleep Storm took an ice pick and poked him three times in his heart and twice in his brain it happen so fast and sudden he tried to get up but due to the injuries he fell straight to the floor as Storm literally stabbed him up a hundred plus times left him for dead laying in his own blood dying. Storm immediately snatched up all her belongings fleeing the scene. Storm couldn't believe that she had just killed a man, but that was her premeditated plan before she came.....

She sat in the house for days confused and not knowing what to do.....

After several days Homicide detectives pulled up to her house, as she looked out of the window clutching her 5 shot .38 that she'd purchased from a crack head for a little of nothing previously in life. As homicide detective approached the stairs before they could even get a chance to put one foot on the stairs she ran out and opened fire on the four detectives unloading all five shots she hit the detectives with three of the bullets neither detective was wounded, because they had on bullet proof vest. They immediately upped their guns shooting her six times one bullet hit her in her left eye going to her brain instantly putting her to death, no longer breathing not one single breath.....

What Storm didn't know was that she wasn't even a suspect and never would've been a suspect she was only getting ready to be questioned about possible suspects on Sidney's murder. She assumed they was coming to get her for the murder oh how she was wrong.....

Storm how you'd be missed we shall forever mourn, we still have visions of you as a kid as you wanted a pony, a unicorn lovely as life as the day you was born.

The daughter of king, princess Storm.....

Upcoming book By Alan Hines

Scandalous Scandals

CHAPTER 1

A
s Prince's song Scandalous slightly echoed in the room at a low pleasant tone through the surround sound speakers, as he constantly inhaled and exhaled the blunt filled with loud, relaxing he could visualize good things to be, making more money,

and growth and development in the drug game.

And then he heard a knock on the door.....

Fontane opened the door and there she stood there with a brown trench coat on. Such a radiant beauty looking like a Goddess on Earth.....

Before she could step all the way in the door, in her own silent mind she admired the aroma of the wonderful smell of the loud smoke, as it made her slightly begin to cough.....

"Step in, I wasn't expecting you for another hour or two," Fontane said. "My kids went to sleep early so I decided to come over while they was asleep. You promise you aren't going to tell anybody," she said. "Girl stop playing you know I aint gone tell nobody," Fontane said. "I'm not like these other ho's that's always out here selling pussy, I'm just doing this because my man locked up, and I got bills to pay," she said.....

Without saying another word she stood up off the couch dropped the trench coat, and there she stood as naked as the day she was born. The biggest roundest prettiest titties imaginable she possessed. The pussy was so hairy looked like chinchilla fur. She turned around to show off her big ole ass.

His mouth dropped, and dick got so hard it felt like it was going to bust. He immediately took his clothes off. He wondered if he'd use a rubber or not, within seconds he made up his mind not to, he figured that if he was finna pay for the pussy he might as well get his money worth.....

As both of them was still standing he bent her over as she used her hands on the couch for stability, he forced his dick in her tight wet pussy, and begin fucking the shit out of her as if he was mad at the world.....Within five pumps he nutted unloaded all of it in her guts. She was disappointed, and pleased at the same time that he nutted so fast; she was disappointed because it felt so wonderful and she wanted the pleasure to be endless, but on the flip side she was pleased because she knew her pussy was a bomb in which made him nut quick.....

"Bend down and suck this dick bitch," Fontane said. "Boy watch your mouth," she said in a low soft tone.....

With no hesitation she got on her knees with an aim to please, to him her mouth was fantastic; she'd suck on the dick thoroughly, while strocking it with her right hand all at the same damn time.

In no time flat he was busting nuts down her throat; he couldn't believe it because it was hard for any chick to make him nut by sucking his dick.

He laid her on her back on the couch and begin squeezing and sucking her titties, as if he was breast feeding as she held her own legs up he begin giving her the dick in it's most harsh form as she continuously begged for him to do it harder.....

For hours on and off they performed hardcore sex.....

As it was time to go she put on her high heels and trench coat as he stared, and watched admiring the view.....

"Okay nigga what's the hold up give me my four hundred," she said. "Here, here go six hundred whenever you need some financial assistance please let me know," Fontane said.

She snatched the money out his hand happy as a kid at Christmas time, as she waved at him, and told him bye.....

CHAPTER 2

Fontane begin to feel his phone vibrating. "Hello," Fontane said. "Hello can I speak to to Fontane," Chresha said. "Yeah this me, who is this," Fontane asked? "This is Chresha." "Why do everytime you call me you always ask to speak to me, and you know you calling my phone, I mean do that make any sense to you," Fontane asked? "Because I know sometimes you be having other people answer your phone," Chresha said. "Girl you know aint nobody answering my phone," Fontane said. "Why do you always ask who this is calling you, what you got another girlfriend or something," Chresha said. "You know damn well I'm not fucking with nobody but you," Fontane said. "Good game, real phony," she said.....

"I've been missing you and shit lately, you must got another bitch because you don't spend no time with me," Chresha said. "You know me I've been traveling state to state doing business ventures," Fontane said. "Business ventures my ass, you been traveling state to state to buy dope," Chresha said. "Is you done lost your motherfucking mind, you can't be saying shit like that over the phone, the feds could have my phone tapped," Fontane said. "Nigga you aint on shit, the feds aint thinking about you, you aint moving enough product," Chresha said.....

Little did she know he was moving more than enough product for the Feds to be watching. His connect in Chicago was supplying him with enough dope to supply a third of Flint city.....

"I'm serious Chresha you gotta be careful of what you say over the phone cuz the Feds can popp a nigga ass for little petty shit they say over the phone. They'll have my ass way in the basement in the Feds joint across country, some motherfucking where," Fontane said.

"Well since you say I haven't been spending that much time with you, why don't you come over now, and wear one of them new lingerie sets under your clothes," Fontane said. "Which one you want me to wear," Chresha asked? "It don't matter just pick one of the newest ones," Fontane said. "A'ight I got you, I'm going to bring my sister with me," Chresha said. "For what," he asked with authority.....He hated her twin sister Teressa with a passion.

"I want to bring her over to do what you've been asking me to do," Chresha said. "What's that," he asked? "You know what you've been wanting me to do," Chresha said.

"What's that," Fontane asked again? "The threesome," she respond.....

His mouth dropped as he dropped the phone on the floor.....

He picked up the phone and immediately asked, "are you serious." "Yeah I'm serious we wanna do it," Chresha said.

"You trying to tell me that as much as me and your sister can't stand each other she wants me to fuck her," he said. "Yes, that's exactly what I'm saying," she said.....

Fontane paused for a minute in disbelief, and overjoyed that he was going to have a threesome with two twin sisters.

"A'ight, ya'll come on over here and bring some drinks with ya'll," Fontane said.

He went into the room popped a Viagara he stole from his grandfather, and an x-pill,

and then fired up a leaf joint. He rushed smoking his leaf joint; he was a closet leaf smoker he didn't want nobody to know he smoked leaf.....

Fontane sat back high as kite visualizing how beautiful the girls look; The twins looked just alike, short, thick ass hell, caramel complexion, smooth skin, dark brown eyes.....

In no time flat the girls were at his house; it seemed like they flew a private jet over there, because they came so fast.

The door bell ring twice; Fontane went to the door looked out his peep hole and to his surprise the girls were standing there. Like damn how they get over here that quick, he thought to himself.

He immediately opened the door before he could say a word Chresha put her index finger to her lips to sush him.

As Chresha and Teressa entered his home, Chresha locked the door. Both women grabbed him by each one of his hands and led him into his bedroom.

Inside Fontane felt like a kid again on the verge of it being his first time getting some pussy.

Within seconds both girls were in their birthday suits standing side by side each other, awaiting for him to undress and give out orders.

Fontane undressed and got on his knees on the bed; he ordered Chresha to suck his dick. Chresha got on the bed on all fours and begin sucking the shit out of his dick.

Teressa begin finger fucking Chresha ass and pussy with two fingers in each hole, right hand fingers in the pussy hole, left hand fingers in the asshole. Fontane couldn't believe what was taking place.

As Fontane was on the verge of busting a nut Teressa begin eating Chresha's pussy in which made his nut burst out like an erupting Volcano.

Fontane begin thinking to himself, these ho's done did this shit before; why they didn't been do this with me. These ho's some freaks doing insence, and everything.

Once Teressa completed eating Chresha out momentarily, Fontane told her to lay on the bed. She laid on the bed flat on her stomach as Fontane begin stuffing his dick in and out her pussy. Teressa laid on the bed watching them while sucking on the two fingers that she'd stuck in Chresha's ass while finger fucking herself with two fingers from her other hand.

Just when Fontane was getting ready to nut he told Teressa, "take your fingers outta your mouth and give me a kiss."

while Fontane and Teressa tongues intertwine she continued fingering herself as Fontane commence to stuff his dick into Chresha pussy.

Fontane then told Teressa to lay flat on her stomach as he begin to enter Teressa he could feel a big difference from Chresha; Teressa's pussy was much tighter, and moist. Now was his chance to take out all his anger, frustration, and dislike for Teressa out on her pussy.

He shoved his dick in her with force, and commenced to fucking her like he was mad at the world. She pleaded for him to stop as he continued going, giving her the dick in it's rawest form.

Once he unloaded his sperm cells in her she jumped up yelling, "I told you to stop." He grabbed her head and begin tongue kissing her, the kiss kinda put her at ease.

After he finished kissing Teressa he started kissing Chresha. Then Chresha and Teressa begin kissing one another.....

As Fontane maintained his composure, deep down within he was going wild inside.....

For hours into the morning came around without to many intermissions they fucked and sucked one another.....

As the night turned into morning all three sat and watched the sun rise will listening to Jazz at a low tone. They laughed and talked reminiscing about last night making plans to do it again.

They ended up showering seperately as everybody went their seperate ways; but right before they left the house Fontane told them, "I'm a call ya'll later on." "Make sure you do," Chresha said.

He hugged both girls and they left, and went their seperate ways.

Fontane fired up a Newport Long and got on the phone to call his guy Rob.....

"Rob guess who I fucked last night," Fontane said. "Who is this," Rob asked? "This Fontane, guess who I fucked last night," Fontane said. "Who," Rob asked? "I fucked Chresha and Teressa together," Fontane said. "No you didn't, get your ass outta here," Rob said. "On my momma I fucked Chresha, and Teressa, and they fucked each other," Fontane said. "Straight up, did they," Rob said. "Yup," Fontane said. "How you pull that off you must of paid for that," Rob said? "Naw I didn't pay, shiit I would've thou," Fontane said, as they both begin laughing.....

"I've been sweating Chresha to have a threesome with me and another woman for a long ass time. So yesterday she call me on some emotional shit talking about we aint been spending very much time together, and some other ole goofy ass shit she was talking about. So I told her to come on over to my crib. She tells me that her and Teressa wanted to do a threesome. At first I thought she was bullshitting because Teressa and me can't stand each other. Come to find out she wasn't bullshitting. They came straight over and got to work. Them ho's done did that shit before," Fontane said. "When you gonna set them out to the guys," Rob asked? "Not yet later," Fontane said. "Why not know instead of later," Rob asked? "I already know how they is it's gonna take a while for them to do it with somebody else," Fontane said.....

Fontane was lying he didn't wanna set them out, he loved Chresha.

"A man I gotta go to the cleaner's, I'll catch up with you later on," Fontane said. "A'ight man I holler at you, love nigga," Rob said. "Love," Fontane said.

Later on that night Fontane cell phone rang.....

"Hello," Fontane said. "I thought you said you was gonna call us," Chresha said. "I got caught in some business deals, other than that I would've call," Fontane said. "Come over here tonight me and Teressa wanna see you, and spend some time with you," Chresha said. "I can't I'm in the middle of some business right now, other than that I'll be there; I promise I'll be over there tomorrow for sho," Fontane said. "I gotta work tomorrow," Chresha said. "Well I'll come over there after work, but before I hang up what made you, and Teressa wanna do that with me," Fontane asked? "I love you, and shit and I'll do anything for you," Teressa said.....

Fontane remained quiet for a seconds pleased with her answer made him feel like a player.....

"But what made Teressa wanna do that," Fontane asked? "She really like you," Chresha said. "Now you know damn well me and Teressa can't stand each other," Fontane said. "That's what you thought, she always liked you," Chresha said. "Be for real, Teressa is the only person I ever met that I argue with everytime we're around," Fontane said. "You just didn't know deep down inside, she liked you, and always wanted to give you some of that pussy," Chresha said.....

Fontane paused for the matter of seconds letting it mirinate in his head.....oh well fuck it if they wanna have threesomes who gives a fuck if she likes me or not, Fontane thought to himself.....

"But uhhh anyway tell Teressa I said, what's up," Fontane said. "A'ight," Chresha said. "I gotta go," Fontane said. "Promise you'll be over here tomorrow when I get off work," Chresha said. "I promise," Fontane said. "I love you," Chresha said. "A'ight I'll holla," Fontane said as the both ended their call.....

The next day Fontane came over and picked up Teressa while Chresha was at work. He took her shopping spent five hundred on 2 pair of high heel shoes.....

Afterwards they went to the show. Once the movie was over they road around town ended up naked, sexing at a sleazy motel.....

Teressa, and Chresha lived together. Once he took Teressa home he had a long talk with her. "Teressa now you know what goes on between me and you stays between me and you," Fontane said. "What do you mean by that," Teressa asked? "Whatever we do when Chresha aint around is between you, and I," Fontane said. "You know damn well I aint no dummy, I aint gonna tell Chresha that we fucked and you took me shopping when she wasn't around, let me tell you a little secret," Teressa said. "What's that," Fontane asked? "I always liked your stanking ass," Teressa said. "You showl gotta a way with showing people you like them," Fontane said. "That's just the way I am, I'm snotty as hell; well anyway let's not bring up old shit," Teressa said.....

She begin to smile genuinely as if she was happy than she ever been in life.....

"You know me and my sister will do anything for you. Whatever we can do to make you happy we're all for it, seeing you happy will only make us more happier," Teressa said.....

He slowly moved his face towards hers as their tongues collided, as he was trying to kiss her, and suck her lips and tongue all at once.

He then stood her up pulled her pants down to her knees. Then pulled his pants down to his knees, bent her over and gave her the dick hardcore in the rawest form.....

Afterwards they sat down and watched some midget porn until they dosed off and went to sleep.....

By the time Chresha came in from work Teressa, and Fontane were fully dressed sound asleep on the couch.....

Chresha walked through the door seen him on the couch and instantly began smiling.....

Chresha walked slowly over to him, dropped her purse took off all her clothes, and laid them on the floor.

She tapped him gently on his head..... "Wake up sleepy head," Chresha said.

He opened his eyes as his vision was a little blurry.

Once his sight became clearer he came to focus on Chresha standing up ass hole naked.

She put her index finger on her lips to ssssh him. Grabbed his hand and led him into the bedroom. She gently closed the door and locked it, got on her knees unbutton, and unzipped his pants grabbed his dick firmly and commenced in attempts to suck the skin off it.

In the process of sucking his dick she could taste and smell pussy; right than and there she knew him and Teressa was fucking while she was at work. she had no problem with it nor was she going to comfront him about it, she figured fuck it let him have his fun.

As he begin squirting his nut down her throat she swallowed it all.....

"Stand up and bend over," Fontane said.....

He pulled his pants to his knees and begin giving her every inch of his dick as she turned her face towards him as is she was looking at him, but in reality she wasn't her eyes was closed. He enjoyed the pleasure of the sight of her ass jiggling, and seeing her fuck faces.

As he begin to nut it felt like the best nut he'd ever released in life, it felt good.

After sexing Chresha went and showered and dressed and woke Teressa up as the three of them went on there expedition of a day, and night filled with excitement.

They kicked it like they were celebrating some sort of victory.....

They started of by simply riding down town area popping bottles as Chresha and Teressa flashed their breast to pedestrians.

They ended up at a dance club.

As they walked in the dance club it was as if they were the center of attraction,

as Jay Rule remake of Stevie Wonder's song Giving It Up echoed in the speakers they begin dancing on the dance floor as if they owned it.

They got so drunk at the club that Teressa forgot were she was at.

Bottles after bottles, going back and forth to the dance floor, and to the photographer taking pictures all night.

They even found a way to take a few puffs of a little weed in the midst of the of all the cigarette smoke, without security catching them.

That night seemed as if all them became closer to one another.....

On their way home from the club they listened to continious 2Pac CD's in a mildly tone while reminiscing about all the fun times they had over time with, and without each other.

Once they made it to Chresha, and Teressa house Teressa and Fontane went straight to sleep, because they was so intoxicated.

Chresha undressed Fontane and Teressa. She took turns sucking on Fontane's dick, and eating Teressa's pussy until she got tired and went to sleep herself.....

After that night Fontane and the girls became real close.

Fontane even stop hanging out with the guys alot because he begin to fall in love with the girls, they had him sprung.

They girls even begin to help Fontane conduct his drug business.

CHAPTER 3

Fontane's connect in Chicago started flooding him with more, and more cocaine; the happiness of love through financial gain came to life, became.

Fontane's connect would supply him with some of the purest cocaine around town.

Each day Fontane started to make more and more money than he'd normally make.

Fontane didn't sell no petty nickels and dimes he sold straight weight.

The more money he made the more money the girls were able to enjoy of his.

The twins would go shopping when ever they got ready. They both had numerous cars eqipped with rims, sounds, and Lamborghini doors.

Fontane really loved the girls and would do anything for them.

The twins on the other hand didn't give a fuck about him, they never did.

The only thing they cared about was more dollar signs.

These ho's stop working they had it made.

That was the only reason they started fucking with him in the beginning was to trick him outta all his doe.

They plan was to both begin sexing him, get him to trust them, and trick him into falling in love to benefit off his wealth, and their plan worked.

These ho's had more game than Milton Bradley. They was thorough in the way they schemed for money.

Only eighteen but had more game then the average women twice their age.

Their game came from all the things they heard and seen. They had enough game to turn filthy animals clean. They could talk preachers into being sinners, turn losers to winners.

Their mom and dad was drug addicts, the rest of their small family was caught up living their own lives, and really didn't give a fuck about the twins. So at an early age the twins had to scheme for money to survive, and they did it well.

It's a sad repition cycle of broken homes, shattered black family structure contrary to the past times of our lives, of days, lives of yesterday, when blacks lived in two parent homes, only addictions was worshipping God within a sense pleasurable tone.....

Throughout sex they'd take him places he never been before. Not just physically but mentally as well. Those ho's had mastered the art of seduction.

These ho's was something else.

Although these ho's was only eighteen they looked every bit of twenty five.

They looked like super models. You'd see them and couldn't tell they was ghetto at all.

They was beautiful, lovely and free as artwork of paintings from God to be mutual.

Many men would stop and stare imagining if they could have atleast one to love frequently suitable.

The twins stood 5.5 and gorgeous enough to give sight to the blind. Smooth caramel skin with caramel brown eyes to match. They wore no make up because they was naturally beautiful.

The twins were identical, other difference was they wore different hair styles. They always kept their hair down, lips juiced up, and nails, and toes done.

The twins made Fontane feel supreme like a emperor or a king; on top of the world above the clouds as it seems, fairy tale turned to reality formulated from a sweet dream.....

CHAPTER 4

More and more for Fontane clientale blossomed grew. More money that was being made Fontane was enjoying life as far as going out clubbing and having fun.

One night Fontane was already high as the clouds that descend in the sky on this place formally known as Earth, he decided to go to a club in which his homie Snake invited him to earlier the same week.

Once he made in the club as if he was stuck in his pleasure mode of time, although their were many others of course in the club it seems as if Fontane was in a world of his own.....

It took him a little while to find Snake but once he did it brought joy to Snake seeing Fontane there as they begin smiling at one another.....

Fontane stepped to Snake, Snake hugged Fontane firmly as if he hadn't seen him within the ages of time.

Snake spoke in Fontane's ear, "it's good to see you", Fontane spoke in Snake's ear, "it's good to see you to". They both had to shout loud because the music was at an all time high.

Snake popped open a bottle of Champagne as it splashed all over Fontane's shirt. Snake tried to apologize but Fontane didn't give a fuck.

"Damn nigga I want Champagne in my glass, not on my shirt," Fontane said as they begin laughing. "Nigga you look like you already wasted." Snake said.

Snake drunk Champagne straight out the bottle, passed it to Fontane as he drunk straight out the bottle as well.

Fontane and Snake went to the dance floor and danced with damn near half the chicks on the dance floor, showing out acting a fool with it.

Within a couple of hours Fontane was to drunk to continue partying.....

"Hey man I'm finna call it a night man, I'll get up with you tomorrow," Fonatne said. "The night just begun," Snake said. "Maybe for you, but I'm finna go home," Fontane said. "So which ho you gonna take home with you," Snake asked? "Nam one I'm finna go home and go to sleep," Fontane said. "Do you want me to drop you off at home," Snake asked? "Naw man I'm cool," Fontane said. "You sure man, you know it's plenty of family members here I can have one of them drop you off, Lord knows you don't need no D.U.I.'s, I'd hate for something to happen to you," Snake said. "Naw B I'm straight, trust me," Fontane said.

As Fontane left the club Snake stared at him, thinking to himself I shouldn't let this drunk ass nigga drive home by himself he might have an accident or something.

Once Fontane left the club Snake continued to party as if this was his last day on Earth.....

On the ride home Fontane felt himself getting ready to throw up; he instantly pulled over, opened the door as he remained seated he bent over and begin throwing up. Outta nowhere a gun man came and shot him three times in the back his head, and one in the neck. Took his life line from him never got a chance to see who done it.....

As the cops arrived, yellow tape to the perimeter; they begun their investigation only witness was homeless man he said the only thing he knew was that he heard gun shots, and seen firely sparks from a gun but didn't see who done it. The police continued to question the homeless man asking him how could he see firely sparks come from a gun but didn't see who did the killing; the homeless man continue to contend that he didn't see who did the killing which was the truth.....

Years later homicide never ever found the killer. Fontane's own guys couldn't find the killer didn't even know who did it and why.....

A week after Fontane was killed his funeral was held the twins sat in the front row crying Crocodile tears; in reality they wasn't crying because Fontane was dead they was crying because Fontane was their financial support.

Snake sat in the back of the church feeling guilty remaining silent, in his own silent mind it felt it was his fault. I knew I should'nt have let Fontane go home by himself, Snake thought to himself.

As the line proceeded to view Fontane's dead body Fontane's momma went to the casket and begin fixing Fontane's suit collar, and begin hollering in Fontane's face. "Why him, why, why, why, him. Why ya'll have to take my son. I hope whomever did this shit die a thousands deaths," she said as tears dripped down her face like the flowing of pouring rain and pain.

One of Fontane's homies grabbed Fontane's mom hugged her and told her Fontane is going to a better place.

"Bitch take your nasty ass hands off me," Fontane's mom said as she slapped him and spit in his face.

"It's cause of you bitches my son is died. If he wouldn't been fucking around the B.D.'s my son would still be living.....

She ran to the middle of the church took off all her clothes upped a box cuter, and said I hope all you bitches die me and my son we lived in this world together, and we shall die together; right then and there she slide her own throat hideously taking her own life away. As suicide is an unforgiving sin she'll never reach the pearly gates within the sky. The box cuter fell to the ground as blood ran from her neck she stumbled momentarily than fell to the ground as the crowds came to her rescue.

They rushed her to the hospital she was pronounced dead on arrival.

After they found she was dead they went back to Fontane's funeral and took his body to be buried.....

A week later Fontane's mom funeral was held at the same church. They buried Fontane's mom right next to Fontane.

Family members and friends never stop grieving over the loss of Fontane and his mom; it was like a mental torture chamber of pain.....

CHAPTER 5

L ife goes on..... Although Fontane was no longer living Fontane's guys was living lovely they surpassed Fontane's success of getting money when he was living. Fontane's team continued to sell only weight; but they wouldn't sell anything less than a quarter ki.....

Snake was the one doing most of the going back and forth to Chicago coping work.

Snake had been dealing with this guy Fly from Chicago on a business level and a personal level.

One day Snake and Fly was kicking it over the phone making arrangements for when Snake would be coming back to Chicago.....

"Hey man whenever you come back to Chicago I need some major assistance from you," Fly said. "What you need man, I'll be up there tomorrow," Snake said. "I'll holler at you then," Fly said. "A'ight be cool man, I'll see you tomorrow," Snake said "You be cool to," Fly said as they both hung up the phone.

The next day when Snake made it to Chicago Fly told him that he had cousin named Roland that was one the run from the police, and could he hide him out in Flint. Of course Snake agreed. Fly told him he'd send his cousin on the Greyhound the following day. They completed their business transactions and Snake made his way back to the city with Kilo's in the trunk.....

The next day Fly called Snake and told him Roland would be pulling up in the bus station shortly, and fly explained to Snake what Roland would be wearing.

Snake set in his car awaiting for Roland to come out; Roland came out as Snake recognized, Snake begin dying laughing.

Roland was like 5.2 wearing the thickest nerdy glasses known to men, and an outfit that looked like it belong to Carlton off Fresh Prince of Bel Air, with a book bag over his back.

Snake automatically knew it was him because Fly had described him to a tee. Roland already knew how Snake looked cause Fly described him to a tee as well.

Snake stepped out of the car still laughing and asked him, "you Roland"? Roland reached out his hand to shake Snake's hand and answered yes I am Roland. "How are you doing sir," Roland said.

This nigga sound like a straight lame, Snake thought to himself.

"I'm doing alright," Snake said.

"How did you know which individual was me", Roland asked? "Fly described you to me vividly. My car is parked over there," Snake said as he pointed to his car.

As Snake turned the key to the ignition Chingy song featuring Tyrese came on every time I try to leave something keep calling me back.

As they begun on their drive to Snake house, Snake blazed up a fat ass blunt filled with dro.

Snake inhaled, and exhaled the smoke vigourously exhaling it from his nose.

Roland begin to let the window down and begin to slightly choke.

After a few hits of the blunt Snake tried to pass it to Roland. "No thank you, I don't smoke, sorry to be a burden but can you raise down your window," Roland asked? "Don't worry about it I'll just put the blunt out," Snake said.

"Thanks man for allowing me to live with you to avoid the trouble I got into in Chicago," Roland said. "If you don't mind me asking what kind of trouble did you get into," Snake asked? "It's a long story," Roland said. "I like long stories," Snake said. "I'll tell you later," Roland said.....

Previous book published by Alan Hines

Book Writer

CHAPTER 1

S uzie and Carl sat at the table using dope.

"How many more bags of dope we got left," Carl asked Suzie while scratching and nodding all at the same time. "We got five mo bags of dope, why you didn't bring no rocks back so I can smoke me some primos," Suzie asked? "I couldn't the joint got hot the nigga who was working the rock packs disappeared, the only reason I brought some dope home is because every time I sold a blow jab, I kept me a couple blows for myself instead of selling them, I'm glad I did cuz the nigga who was working the blow jab disappeared to when the police came through. I know they wondering where the fuck I'm at I was supposed to work for the rest of the day, I'm just gone tell them I left cuz some police came through that had locked me up before," Carl said.

Carl continued scratching and nodding as if he was sleep for a few seconds. He slightly opened his eyes and looked up at Suzie.....

"This dope a bomb, this dope better than the dope they had yesterday," Carl said. "Yeah I know I think they put some new shit on the dope, whatever they putting on it they need to keep putting it on it," Suzie said.

Carl upped his dick.....

"Bitch suck this dick," Carl said. "I told you about calling me out my name, put your dick up before Latisha come in," Suzie said. "Aw yeah I forget she was in there, I'm glad she didn't walk in here while I had my dick out," Carl said.....

Ten seconds later in comes Latisha.....

"Mom I'm hungry give me some money so I can get me something to eat," Latisha said. "Girl I brought you something to eat yesterday," Suzie said. "But that was yesterday, what I only supposed to eat once a week," Latisha said. "Girl don't be getting smart at the mouth. I wish I would've listen to my momma and got an abortion when I was pregnant with you," Suzie said.

"Here girl here go ten dollars, and bring me some candy back," Suzie said.

Every time this bitch get high she always want to suck on some candy, Latisha thought to herself.

On her way to the store she ran into one of her little friends Jennifer.....

"Where are you going Latisha," Jennifer asked? "I'm on my way to the store to get my dope fiend ass momma some candy," Latisha said. "Why do dope fiends always gotta have candy when they get high off dope," Jennifer asked? "I don't know, I be wondering the same thing," Latisha said.

"My birthday is tomorrow," Jennifer said. "My birthday is in a couple of weeks," Latisha said. "Fo real," Jennifer said. "Fo real, I'll be eleven," Latisha said. "I'll be twelve," Jennifer said.

"Let me go get my momma this candy, cuz this bitch gone be tripping if it take me to long to come back with her candy," Latisha said. "Stop by here when you come back," Jennifer said. "A'ight," Latisha said.....

As Latisha made it within the store she noticed that all three lines were long as hell.

She went into the section where the candy was.....

What should I get candy bars, or jolly ranchers, fuck it I'll get one of each, Latisha thought to herself.

She went to get in a long ass line to pay for the candy.....

While waiting in line she begin to think about what was she going to order from the restaurant next door.....

I'mma order me a cheese burger, fries, and a slurpy, she thought to herself.....

The line continued to move slow.....

I'm tired of waiting in this line, Latisha thought to herself.....

Without no hesitation she put the candy bar, and jolly rancher in her pocket. She figured she'd steal the candy and keep all the money for herself.

She stepped outta line and begin walking towards the door.....

"Hey little girl wait, wait," the Arab lady said.

Latisha got nervous and tried to run outta the store.

A shot came from a .357 hit Latisha in the back.

Little Latisha never seen the gun, she just heard the shot, and felt the bullet. Her body couldn't take it she shook, and drop as the sound of the gun was like an echo as everyone in the store begin yelling, and screaming and running outta the store.....

The Arab man grabbed the gun from his wife.

"What made you do that," he asked? "I didn't do it purpose it was a mistake I pointed the gun at her just to scare her and it went off," the Arab lady said.....

The Arab man walked over and looked at the little girl lying there in her own blood. In his own silent mind he prayed to Allah that she wasn't dead. Swiftly visions of his very own little girl lying there shot and bleeding raced through his head.....

"I hope she aint dead," he said. "Go, go, get in the car and drive away," he said. "Where to," she asked? "Go to my friends Whola's house he got a private jet tell him to take you back to

Saudia Arabia. Here take this gun to, and give it to Abdula and tell him I said dispose of it, he'll know what to do with it," he said.....

As she ran out the back door to her car, he ran to lock the front doors, and the back door behind her. He went to get all the surveillance videos, ran out the back door up the alley to throw the DVD's in the garbage, ran back into the store locked the back door swiftly.

Dialed 911 and told the police a little girl just got shot, and that he needed an ambulance right now. Little did he know someone had already called the police, they were already on their way.

Once the police and the paramedics arrived one paramedic checked Latisha's pulse and seen that she was still living.

Abdula felt a momentary sign of relief knowing that, that little girl was alive.

The ambulance rushed Latisha to the hospital.

He told the police his version of the story. Then they asked for the surveillance videos. He told them that he didn't have any because his surveillance system was broke.

The police continued to search for shell casings or any other type of physical evidence, none was found.

Some of the officer went outside across the street to the crowd, and got a statement for someone that was actually in the store when the incident occurred.....

After many hours searching for evidence the police escorted Abdula to the police station so he could file a police report. As they walked out the store once Abdula finished properly locking the front door they walked towards the police car as one female out of the crowd from across the street yelled out, "bitch I hope you die."

One black detective paused looked over at her curiously wondering why did she make that outburst.

So they continued on to the police station once they made it there it was seven other people there that was in the store when the shooting occurred getting reports filed.

The police surrounded Abdula and escorted him to the interrogation room way in the back. All the officer left him in the room by himself. Through the glass Abdula seen all the officers talking amongst themselves he couldn't hear what they were saying through the door that was closed and that had real thick glass.

Abdula noticed how the big black officer face was in shock as the other officers talked.

Majority of the officers left the hallway and went to various areas in police station as the big black officer and a little short fat white officer stayed in the hallway talking.

Eventually the white officer spent off as the black officer entered the room smiling.....

"So you say three men was robbing your store, as the little girl tried to run out the door one of the men shot her in the back, correct," the black officer said. "Yes, that's correct," Abdula said. "Three black guys right," the black officer said. "Right," Abdula said.

The black officer started to smile harder than before.....

"We got eight people, one by the store, and seven people in station right now as we speak saying that your wife shot that lil girl," the black officer said. "That's a lie, why would my wife shoot a little girl," Abdula said.....

The black officer gave no reply but handcuffed Abdula.....

For hours different officers tried to get Abdula to tell the truth about what had happen but Abdula stuck to his story.....

Abdula was placed in a holding cell, as they went on a manhunt for his wife.....

Somebody went back and told everybody from the hood that Abdula told the police a lie that a nigga shot Latisha instead his wife. People from the hood begin to uproar.....

Later that night Latisha's auntie walk up with her heavy make-up damaged from a over flow of tears. She walked up to some the guys standing on the corner felt to her knees and begin crying loudly.....

"She didn't make it, God took my baby away from me," Latisha's aunt said.....

A lot of people from the hood including Latisha's family just blanked out. First they went to Abdula's store and set fire to it. Then they went to each every Arab business in the hood, and fucked them up, damn near killed two Arabs. Burning down all their businesses to the ground; they pour gasoline on one Arab and set him on fire, damn near killed him to, but he saved his own life by using the stop, drop, and roll method once they left.....

It's was hard for the police to contain the violence that night.....

For a couple of days to follow people from the hood, as well as homicide would search for Abdula's wife, she was nowhere to be found....

Three days after Latisha was shot, and killed Abdula was charged with conspiracy to commit murder. Homicide rigged it up as if he told his wife to do it.....

Abdula was sent to the county jail, and given a high bond because he was a flight risk. His bond was set at a hundred thousand to walk. A hundred thousand wasn't shit to him he owned other stores and a few apartment buildings. He bonded out the same day.....

About a week after Latisha was killed, and buried niggas from the hood was tired of looking for Abdula's wife, but became even thirstier to find Abdula's wife to take her life away as she did Latisha.....

It was this young nigga that was sixteen named Twon whom inner soul had been crying out since Latisha's death; he cried out feeling like why, why this little girl Latisha had to die.....

Unexpectedly Twon had heard that Abdula had a store on the other side of town.....

The next morning Twon, and two of his guys got strapped, and went to the store early in the morning before it even opened looking for Abdula's wife or one of Abdula's family members. To his surprise there Abdula was opening up his store, he couldn't believe it he thought Abdula was still in jail. They pulled up the block and parked.....

"Man let's just rush up on him, and make him show us where his wife is," Twon said. "Be for real you think he just gone tell us where his wife is at," Q said. "People tend to do a lot of things that they wouldn't normally do once they got a big ass gun in their face," Twon said. "He aint gonna tell you where his wife at," John, John said with confidence. "We still gotta try," Twon said. "Fam, it's broad daylight man, you just wanna walk up and up guns on him," Q said. "What the fuck did we get strapped and come over here for," Twon ask? "We need to stake out the store first," John, John said. "You sound like a nerdy college motherfucker, one of them white boys, we need to stake out the store first. You niggas is stupid, we come all the way over here to gets down and you niggas act like ya'll scared. This nigga wife done killed this little girl, shot her to death for no reason. That's one thing about death aint no coming back from that shit once you die it's over. You know what, fuck ya'll niggas, on my life," Twon said.....

Twon bailed out of the car walked up to Abdula upped on him made him finish opening up the store walked him in made him get on his knees, slid his throat with a razor then shot him in the head once execution style and left the store.

Twon came running out the store with the razor in his left hand, and the gun in his right hand, bailed in the car pulled off.....

As they rode, destination to the hood Q and John, John remained silent as Twon talked and kicked it like nothing never happen.....

In reality Twon was going to walk Abdula into the store to force him to tell him where his wife was at, and for him to take him to his wife; but once he got in the store visions of Latisha laying in a casket begin flashing in his head which provoked him to take away Abdula's life.....

A couple of weeks later Twon was having a small birthday party for his seventeen birthday at a tavern in the hood. Outta nowhere homicide rushed in placed him under arrest Twon had no idea of what was going on, and he wondered to himself which murder were they grabbing him for cuz he had been doing so much dirt. He would've never guessed that it was the murder of Abdula.....

Homicide probably would've never grabbed or even suspected him over that murder if Q and John, John wouldn't never went back to hood and told people. Q and John, John only told a few people, but those few people told a few more people, and those few more people told a few more people and word of mouth slowly spreaded.....

Some nigga from the hood was getting hassled from the police for some other shit, and gave up information about Twon killing Abdula so they would let him free. The police didn't ask the nigga about any unsolved murders, but he knew that if he gave them that lead that they'd definitely let him go and forget about the petty shit they was harassing him for, and it worked.....

Once they made it to the police station Twon came to find out they had a witness whom lived across the street from the store seen him and that they had surveillance from the store that showed him killing Abdula.

What Twon didn't know was that by him having his hoody on with the strings slightly tied around his mouth, and hade his head down majority of the time during the incident that the witness nor the surveillance really couldn't actually say, or show it was him.....

They put Twon in a line up in order for the one witness to positively I.D. him, and she did point him out that was only because he was a real short guy, everybody else in the lineup was tall.

Twon always thought line ups were only in movies but he came to see that the police do that for real.....

They shipped Twon to the county and charged him with Abdula's murder. Gave him a high ass bond so Twon knew he wasn't going to bond out.....

This was Twon first time to the county he had only been to juvenile detention once now that he was seventeen there was no more juvenile for him he had to be with the grown men.

Once he made it to the Cook county jail, division 10 he was screened to see if he was gang affiliated, he was an UnderTaker ViceLord. He got introduced to the other ViceLords, they gave him a little cosmetics, and food. They offered squares, but he didn't smoke. Afterwards they laid out to him the security measurements.....

His first day on the deck was average.....

Twon immediately noticed that the county was totally different from the juvenile detention center in many different ways.....

On his third day of being in jail he awoke from the sounds the doors being unlocked to eat breakfast.....

I can't believe I'm stuck in jail for a body, he thought to his self as he walked to go get his tray.....

They had scrambled eggs and oatmeal on the trays. This was his first time eating oatmeal, it was a bomb to him.....

In juvenile they'd go to the lunchroom to eat as school kids did, in the Cook county jail there was no lunchroom in his division, the officers brought the trays to the deck, and two or three assigned inmates passed the trays out to the rest of the people on the deck.

Certain inmates would get special trays that revolved around health issues; like hypro trays, and low fat trays.....

Twon ate his tray went in cell in attempts to go back to sleep.....

Approximately three minutes after Twon laid off in the bunk he heard one nigga say the next time you bitches don't give me my hypro tray we gonna tear this bitch up.

Then one of the niggas that was working the trays yelled out it aint gonna be no next time and hit him in his mouth for calling him a bitch.

In 0.3 seconds the deck went up, he kicked off a riot between the fin ball, and niggas under the six. The fin ball consists of mainly ViceLords, Latin Kings, and Black P-Stones, amongst others. The six mainly consist of G.D's, B.D's, and Latin Folks amongst others.

Twon begin to hear people yelling, the bottom of gym shoes squeaking against the floor.

He jumped out his top bunk to see what was going on, and seen food trays flying back and forth, knives penetrated flesh, as others were getting stumped, and beat.....

Twon was on his way out of the cell, but in 0.3 seconds they niggas under the six, and the niggas under the fin separated, both to each side of the deck, as a standoff.

Twon then seen more knives than he'd seen in kitchen sets.....

Twon cell was in the back where the niggas under six was so he didn't know what to do, he hoped they didn't run in there on him.....

Within no time a gang C/O's ran on the deck to disperse the violence.....

Everybody that had knives tossed them to the ground and ran to their cells as the C/O's came in whupping nigga's and locking them in their cells.

All those that were injured remained out there cells until the paramedics came from the med unit of the county.....

Nigga's from both sides got fucked up real bad, from puncher lungs, to broken jaws, to staples in heads, to stitches in faces.....

The C/O's found twelve knives.....

Twon had heard many bad things about the county before he even made it there, but he never knew that a deck would go up, and niggas get fucked up real bad over a petty hypro tray.....

What Twon didn't know was that the individual working the trays gave the man three regular trays and apologized for not giving him a hypro tray, they gave his tray away to someone else by mistake. The man accepted there apology ate the three regular trays and started talking shit.

This was like a welcoming party to the county jail for Twon.....

They officer in division 10 decided to split up the deck before they let them off lock down.

When they moved him to another deck he was placed in a cell with a Latin King; which was good for him because Latin Kings and ViceLords were under the fin, allies.

His new celli was nicknamed Loco and he lived up to his name. Twon and Loco hit it off immediately.

The division 10 was still on lock down. Each time someone on any deck got stabbed the entire division would go on lockdown.

Twon hadn't got in touch with his family yet because each time he'd call he'd get no answer. Now that he was on lock down he couldn't call at all.

Loco had been locked up for two years fighting a murder. During those two years Loco had caught all type of assaults on inmates, aggravated batteries for stabbing inmates, and UUW for getting caught with a knife.

Loco was the true essence of a gang banger.

As days past Town begin to open up to Loco and tell his story of why he was locked up. Loco took a liking for him knowing that he wasn't a stool penguin to work with the police and sign a statement on John-John, and Q. Loco knew he could've made all three of them ray's on Abdulla's murder, but he kept his mouth shut.

Loco had a personal vendetta for stool penguins, because his rap was turning states on him.....

"Don't worry about your case, just pray to the creator and leave it in his hands. One of the best things to do while you're in her is read. Reading can take your mind into different areas. It's been times where I been reading a book, and forgot I was even in jail, it was like I was one of the characters in the book, real talk," Loco said. "What kind of books should I read," Town asked? "I read almost anything I can get my hands on, me and you two different people, maybe you should read whatever books that's exciting to you, the ones that keep your mind away from the free world. I got a book for you to read, read this," Loco said as he reached under his mattress grabbed a book and handt it to him.

Twon read the title to himself, The Greatest Sex Stories Ever, Volume 1.

"I don't want to read no sex stories," Twon said. "Go ahead this shit a bomb," Loco said.....

Twon got the top bunk opened up the book and started reading it: Chapter 1, Several People.....

Chad and Felicia was a married couple that had been happily married for twenty years. Chad was 43, and Felicia was 50 years of age. Throughout their twenty years of marriage they didn't have too many problems; not once did Chad or Felicia unfaithfully cheat on one another.

Chad and Felicia sex life was average, but they both wanted more excitement.....

Chad worked in an office building around many women, but he'd grew a liking for this eighteen year old young lady that had been working there for only a few months. Her name was Rita. Rita had one of the nicest ass any man would love. Each day at work she'd either wear tight jeans, or a full length tight skirt. On top of her nice ass she had a cute baby doll face.

Each day Chad and Rita would conversate, but nothing outta the ordinary, simply casual conversation.

One day Rita and Chads conversation begin to get a little heated. Rita begin to tell Chad that she'd only been sexually active with one man in her life, her last boyfriend.

By Chad being faithful to his wife he got on to another topic. But in the back of Chad's mind he knew that when a woman told a man such business that was because she was interested in him.....

Twon liked the story, and couldn't put the book down, wanted to see what would happen next, so he continued to read.....

Felicia would go grocery shopping most of the time by herself. She became acquainted with a young man named Micheal that worked at the grocery store.

Micheal was 22 years old and one of the most hansom man Felicia had ever laid eyes upon.

Felicia and Micheal would have casual conversation when she came to the grocery store, but nothing outta the ordinary.

One day when Felicia was leaving the grocery store Micheal told her that she had a nice ass. Felicia couldn't believe what he'd said. She turned around and asked him "what did you just say." "I said you got a nice ass." She begin laughing, and thanked him for the compliment.....

Later on that night Felicia and Chad was watching some stand-up comedy on TV. One of the comedians begin talking about how this younger lady was attracted to him, and of course he made a joke out of it. Chad begin to tell Felicia about that young lady from work that liked him. Felicia begin to tell Chad about the young man from the grocery store that liked her. It was no big deal to either one of them because they had a marriage built of trust.

Before the night end they watched a XXX rated movie. The movie consist of all threesomes. Chad told Felicia he'd like to be involved in a threesome. Felicia told Chad she might if she wasn't married. She didn't want to see her husband having sex with another woman.....

After the movie they sexed throughout the night.....

The next day at work Rita was all over Chad. Chad was intelligent enough to know she wanted sex..... Coincidently on the same exact day Micheal gave Felicia a hug at the grocery store. This wasn't a average hug, this hug was a hug as it was from one lover to another.....

Later that day both Felicia and Chad told each other of their experience with the youngsters. Chad admitted to Felicia that he liked Rita, but could never get involved while he was married to her. Felicia said she felt the same way about Micheal.

Out of nowhere Chad said let's invite them to our bedroom one by one. Felicia begin to blush, while giggling and said no in a phony way. Chad had been with her all these years and knew her no wasn't sincere.

Chad didn't say anything else about a threesome for several days.....

Within the next several days at work Chad begin to get physical with Rita. He even palmed her ass and titties she enjoyed it.

What Rita didn't understand was why he didn't want to creep off and have sex; Chad didn't want to cheat on his wife, the times he palmed her ass and titties was when his dick get hard and he got out of control.....

A day later after he palmed her merchandise they was at work talking about various things. Out of nowhere Chad kissed Rita. After kissing her he told her that he wanted her but didn't want to cheat on his wife. She told him what she don't know won't hurt her.....

Twon begin to really get excited, thinking to himself that they should make a movie out of this shit.....

"I just can't cheat on my wife. I even told her about you and she'd enjoy meeting you. The only way you and I could get together was in a threesome," Chad said.

Chad paused hoping she'd say she wanted to have a threesome that would've been like a dream come true for Chad. As he paused she paused, confused not knowing how to reply.....

"Well in order for me to have a threesome I'd really have to like the man a whole lot to involve myself in that," Rita said.

"Do you really like me," Chad asked? Rita begin to smirk. "You got a valid point because I really do like you a lot. I like that you don't want to cheat on your wife, most men wouldn't turn down pussy married or not. First let me meet your wife and we will see how it goes," Rita said.....

Chad went straight home from work. When he got there Felicia was naked ready for sex, and he gave her sex, great sex.....

After sexing Chad told Felicia all that happen between Rita and himself he left out the part when he palmed her ass and titties. Felicia told him she didn't know about a threesome.....

As days passed along Chad continued to ask Felicia of a threesome. She told him that if we have a threesome it would have to be with another man. Chad told her to let's try it with Rita first.....

"You'd let your wife have sex with another woman," Felicia asked? "Yes if I'm involved," Chad said.....

Felicia remained silent for a little while.....

"Forget it let's give it a try with Rita, but if I don't like it I'm not doing it anymore," Felicia said.....

The next day at work Chad told Rita, "My wife wants to have a threesome with you." "How do you know that she don't even know me," Rita said. "Although she don't know you I've been telling her good things about you. We've been together for twenty years and my wife and I are in love, therefore we do what it takes to make each other happy. This threesome will make all three of us happy," Chad said.....

Later on that day Chad showed up at his home with Rita. Dinner was already ready. All three sat down and ate dinner. While eating dinner Rita and Felicia begin to conversate about girl things, they seemed to be getting along well.

"You look nice," Felicia said to Rita. "I was thinking the same thing about you," Rita said.....

At that very moment Chad knew that they wanted to get it in.

Chad went into the living room and placed on a XXX rated movie; of course the movie was of a sexual threesome. He then called both women in to watch the movie.

To his surprise as they begin watching the movie the girls acted like they couldn't take their eyes off of it.....

In the process of Chad and the girls watching the movie Chad spontaneously upped his dick and told Felicia to suck it. Felicia begin sucking it like never before. It was as she'd studied the art of deep throating.

As Rita sat and watched she was amazed of how long his dick was. Rita was afraid to have his big dick in her little pussy.

As Felicia continued sucking on his dick she looked out the corner of her eyes to see Rita's facial expression. Rita's facial expression looked as if in the back of her mind she was saying hurry up bitch I'm next.

In no time flat Chad begin to bust a nut, he released it in Felicia's face; at that very moment it was as Rita felt like she was releasing her orgasm.....

"Take them panties off," Chad said in a low firm, sensual tone of voice.....

The women didn't say a word as Rita laid on the couch Felicia snatched of Rita's pants, then her panties, then her shirt, and bra. Then Felicia laid on the couch as Rita snatched of all her clothes.....

They both were ready to eat away at each other's pussy but Chad told Felicia to get on all fours. Chad banged Felicia pussy as Rita watched Felicia continuously licked her tongue in and out at Rita while hollering unable to take the dick as usual.....

Chad stop fucking Felicia and told Rita to get on all fours. As he stuck his dick in her she tried to run from it, Felicia held Rita's hands down, as Chad gripped her waist tightly and started slamming his dick in, and out the pussy. Chad couldn't believe how good, wet, and tight her pussy was.

As Rita was hollering Felicia continued to hold her hands down, and kissed her in the mouth, as their tongue connected Rita could feel herself cumming.....

Felicia stop kissing her, but continued to hold her hands down as Rita looked at Felicia with her eyes slightly open breathing heavily, and moaning saying, "oh his dick is too big, his dick is too big, his dick is too big." Felicia kissed her again, and then told her, "Just take it baby."

Chad started banging Rita even harder because he was getting ready to nut, and Rita knew this.....

"Please take it out, and nut my mouth," Rita said.....

Chad took it out, but before he could put his dick in her mouth his nut splashed all across her lips. She liked the nut off her lips, and then licked the nut off his dick, and set on the couch as he stood straight up she begin sucking his dick.

Her mouth is fantastic, Chad thought to himself.

As Rita continued sucking on his dick she could feel Felicia sucking on her titties, and trying stick her hand up her pussy, as Rita tried to control Felicia's hand, as Chad was force feeding her his dick she felt overpowered and bullied, and she loved it.....

Then Chad started eating Rita's pussy while Felicia sucked on his dick, as Felicia fingered her own self all at the same time.

We should've been done a threesome, Felicia thought to herself.....

Then Chad begin eating Felicia's pussy while she ate Rita's pussy, all at the same time.....

Before they even begun sexing Chad just knew that at least one of the girls wouldn't cooperate with some of the sexual acts, oh how he was wrong.

Then Rita got on her knees to suck Chad's dick again while Felicia finger fucked Rita's pussy, and ass at the same time.....

Chad was really enjoying himself, but the girls were enjoying themselves even more.....

All night Felicia, Chad, and Rita sexed thoroughly.....

The next morning all three got into the shower together. Afterwards Felicia went to work. Chad took Rita to her house to change clothes, and then Chad and Rita went to work.....

All day at work they gazed into each other's eyes with lust built within.....

After work he hugged her and told her he'd sat up a date when Felicia, her, and him could hang out, even if she didn't want to sex again. He told her the date would probably be tomorrow.

Both Rita and Chad was in a hurry so they immediately went their separate ways.....

He rushed home from work hoping Felicia was there. He wanted to privately ask her how much she enjoyed intercourse last night.....

Once he made it from work she was there. Soon as he walked through the door she begin tongue kissing him like never before.

Afterwards they sat down, and talked.....

"How did you enjoy the experience last night," he asked? "Last night was wonderful let's do it again tonight," she said.....

He begin to smile knowing that he'd open up this wonderful door of group sex at its best.....

"No we aint going to do it tonight, let's wait a few days, we don't want to seem too eager," he said.....

Right then and there she begin tongue kissing him, and they undressed and fucked for hours.....

Later on that night Felicia begin to tell him about her secret freaky desires. The one freaky desire that fascinated him the most was when she told him she wanted to have sex with a group of only men as they treated her like a cheap hooker. He begin thinking to himself like damn I'm married to a closet freak. He felt good that he'd brought the freaky side outta her.....

The next day at work he walked up to Rita and hugged her liked he hadn't seen her in years, and was happy to see her.....

"Did you enjoy yourself the other night," Chad asked Rita? "Yes I did I aint never felt that good before," Rita said. "Which part did you like the best," Chad asked? "I liked it the best when you, and your wife was taking turns performing oral sex on me, but actually I liked all of it, but when you and her took turns performing oral sex it was a little better than all the rest. I wanted to tell you yesterday, but we didn't do too much talking yesterday," Rita said. "Yeah I felt the same way but I believe that when you and my wife took turns sucking my dick that was the best part for me," Chad said. "Sshhhh, you don't have talk all loud we don't want anybody in our business," Rita said. "Sorry about that," Chad said.....

She then kissed him on the cheek and said, "Thanks for bringing me to life the other night. When are we going to do it again," she asked? "Honestly me and my wife enjoy having you around without sex, but we'd love to have sex with you more often, but it's only one problem," he said as he looked out the window in order for her not to be looking at him face to face. "What's the problem," she asked? "Me and my wife wants you to do everything sexually," he said. "Sure it's not a problem," she said.....

Chad came at her like that to insure that he could have his way with her this time and every other time.....

"Once our day at work is over I'll take you home with me," Chad told her. "Okay that's cool," Rita said.....

Chad and Rita showed up at Chad's home unexpectedly. As they entered the door Felicia couldn't believe it she became overjoyed, instantly smiling and undressing. In 0.7 seconds Felicia was totally naked tongue kissing Rita.

Chad and Rita then undressed. Chad ordered Felicia to suck his dick. Rita just stood there naked watching.

Within minutes Chad bust a nut in Felicia face. He then ordered Rita to suck his dick; she acted like she didn't want to do it, but she got on her knees and did it anyway.....

Chad grabbed the back of her head and begin fucking her face, once he got ready to nut he released it in her mouth.

Chad stood Rita up bent her over and begin fucking her from the back. Chad liked Rita's pussy, it was much tighter than Felicia pussy.

While Chad fucked Rita from the back giving her the dick in the hardest rawest format Felicia stood up watching while fingering her own pussy with her index, and middle finger while sucking on two of her fingers from the other hand.

When it was time for Chad to release his enormous load of nut he let it loose on Rita's ass cheeks as he jagged all of the nut of his dick.....

As Twon continued to read the book he begin to think to himself like damn this shit better than a porn movie. Loco was right reading a good book takes your mind away from being in jail.

The book was so good that Twon actually felt like he was living it himself. He felt like he was married to Felicia, and at that very moment he was the one busting nuts on Rita's ass cheeks.

Twon dick was harder than it ever been reading that sex story.....

Loco laid on the bottom bunk remaining silent knowing what Twon was experiencing off reading the book. Loco knew that this book captivated readers, because the sex scenes were incredible.....

Twon continued to read.....

"Felicia lay on the couch, now Rita stick your tongue as deep in her pussy as you can," Chad said.....

She stuck her tongue in Felicia's pussy, and started eating.....

While she was eating it Chad whispers in Rita's ear.....

"Rita you're doing a great job I'm proud of you. Me and my wife loves you," Chad said.....

Of course Rita knew they didn't really love her but she still liked hearing it.....

"Yes, yes keep eating that pussy just like that," Chad said while fingering Rita's pussy.....

Chad stops fingering Rita and started eating her pussy.

After Rita came twice Chad stuck his dick off in her which made her eat Felicia's pussy even better.....

After Rita was done eating Felicia's pussy, and Chad was done fucking Rita, Chad sat on the couch to relax and take a break. The girls didn't want a break. Rita begin sucking on Chad's dick while Felicia was licking on the crack of Rita's ass.....

After sexing for hours all three showered together and then Felicia and Chad dropped Rita off at home.....

A few days later Felicia begin to ask about Rita because it had been a few days since the last time she'd seen her, and she'd wanted to fuck her again.

Chad would see Rita at work every day, but figured he'd wait a week or two before he brought her home again Chad and Rita had got real close, they'd even start going on lunch breaks together.....

One day while at the grocery store Felicia wasn't even thinking about Micheal, and outta nowhere he approached her looking good as ever. He had a smile on face that would light up the world, and that particular day he'd been to the barber shop.....

"You look good with your new haircut," Felicia said. "Thought I'd try a new look. I haven't seen you shopping in a few days," Micheal said. "That's because I didn't need any groceries until today. How are you doing," she asked? "Well I'm doing alright, tired of this job at the grocery store," he said. "You know you gotta do what you gotta do to pay the bills," she said. "Yeah you right about that," Micheal said.....

"You starting to get thick," Micheal said. "That's your second time making a comment about my ass, keep your eyes off my body parts, I'm married," she said. "But you do have a nice body," he said. "Thanks," she said.

"I can't lie I cherish the moments we share together when you come to the grocery store. Each day I watch the front doors in hopes of you entering one of them. My day isn't complete unless I see you," Micheal said. "Is that right," she said. "To keep it real I wish we could be together all day every day. They stood in the aisle of the grocery store and talked for almost an hour non-stop.

After an hour she purchased her grocerys, as Micheal escorted her to her car.....

Before she knew it she was in Micheal's apartment getting fucked.....

After having sex with Micheal she felt bad that she cheated on her husband. She started to tell Mike how she was feeling inside.....

"Mike I'd been with this man for twenty years and not once did I cheat on him until you came along," she said. "But at least it was with someone who cares about you. He'll never find out about us if things get deeper," Mike said. "It's not the point of him finding out it's the fact that I did cheat on him," she said.....

Felicia laid on Mike's bed with her hand over her face. Mike assumed she was crying, but she wasn't. She was hiding her shame, while mentally going through a thing.

Mike started to eat her pussy to make her feel better, and it worked.....

Later that day Felicia moped around the house.....

"What's wrong you aint been your normal self, all day," Chad said. "It's nothing wrong, I feel good actually," Felicia said. "Stop it, I been knowing you all these years, and I know when something is wrong with you," Chad said. "There's nothing wrong," Felicia said with confidence..... Chad knew she was lying.....

For days Felicia walked around feeling sad.....

Chad knew something was wrong, he decided to take her out to eat, and to a dance club, Felicia loved to dance.....

Once they made it back home Chad hugged Felicia, and held her in his arms, and told her that he loved her, which made Felicia feel even worser.....

Felicia went into the back room and came right back out.....

"I love you, and wouldn't ever want to lose you," Felicia said. "Don't won't too lose me," Chad said. "I got a secret to tell you," Felicia said. "Aw that's why you been all sad for the last few days," Chad said. "It's a problem with me telling you my secret, I don't want to be handt no divorce papers," Felicia said. "I'm your husband you can talk to me about anything," Chad said. "I didn't play fair ball I cheated," Felicia said. "With who," Chad said. "The young guy at the grocery store," She said. "I knew that, that's why you been all sad, and that's why you ask me earlier, what would I do if I was married to a woman and caught her cheating. Well I gotta secret to I been cheating on you with Rita," Chad said.....

Chad began hugging her tightly.....

"I can't believe you're not mad," Felicia said. "Actually I'm glad I married someone like you, how many women you know that would cheat, and then come tell their husband about it, how many women you know that would have a threesome with their husband," Chad said. "Where's Rita," Felicia asked?

Chad began laughing knowing Felicia wanted action.....

"I'll bring her over tomorrow," Chad said. "Thank you, I really need, and want her," Felicia said. "Do you want to have sex with the guy from the grocery store again," Chad asked... Felicia paused before answering the question..... She looked Chad in his eyes, and said yep. Chad gave no remarked, instead he just smiled.

The next day he brought Rita home both Rita and Felicia was so happy to see one another that most of the night they had sex with only one another like he wasn't even there.....

The next day freaky thoughts begin racing through his head.....

"What's the guy named that work at the grocery store," Chad asked? "His name Micheal, I just call him Mike," she said. "Why don't we invite him, and Rita over for dinner, then we can have a foursome," Chad said.....

Felicia begin smiling, and laughing.....

"A foursome I never heard of that before, I can invite him, but I don't know if he'll be interested in coming," she said. "He will be interested in having sex with two women at the same time, trust me," Chad said. "So you going to have sex with another man," Felicia asked? "Hell naw, me and him gone have sex with you, and Rita," Chad said. "Okay I'll go to the grocery store tomorrow to ask him," she said. "Don't you have his phone number," Chad asked? "No," she said. "You rotate with a guy, having sexual intercourse with him, and you don't have his number," Chad said. "No, I only sex with him once when we rotate with each other it's always when I come to the grocery store, I'll see him at the grocery store tomorrow, and I'll ask him," Rita said.....

The next day Chad, and Rita was in Chad's kitchen preparing dinner. All the while, while they were cooking they hoped that Felicia would bring Mike home for the foursome. As the food was done cooking, still nice, and hot they laid it out on the table like a Thanksgiving dinner.

Chad and Rita didn't eat them waiting for Mike, and Felicia. They just sat at the table reminiscing.....

About forty five minutes after the food was done, to Chad, and Rita's surprise in comes Felicia, and Mike. Chad, and Rita was so happy that they jumped straight up out their chairs hugging Mike one by one as if they'd known him all their lives.....

They sat down, and began to eat dinner, as the four of them continued to smile with nasty sexual thoughts running through their heads.....

Felicia got up went to the bathroom, and came back naked as the day she was born. Mike mouth drop knowing it was time for action.....

Chad stood up upped his dick, Felicia got on her knees and began sucking his dick. Mike stood up and watched in amazement.....

Rita got on her knees unzipped Mikes pants, he stuffed his dick in her mouth as she begin sucking on it as if it was a lolly pop.....

Mike watched his own dick go in and out of Rita's mouth feeling the joyous pleasure of what sex brings within this life.....

Her mouth is fantastic, Mike thought to himself.

Mike continues to glance over at Felicia's performance and couldn't wait to get a piece of her.

Outta nowhere Mike felt his dick get harder as the nut exploded in Rita's mouth as Rita swallowed all of it like champ.

Mike couldn't believe Rita made him nut it was hard for a woman to suck his dick and make him nut.....

Mike walked over to Felicia and stood her up, as she was now on her feet bent over still sucking Chad's dick Mike stuffed his dick in her pussy, and begin fucking the shit out of her.....

As they could hear Felicia slightly moaning although Chad dick was on her mouth, Rita begin playing with her own pearl tongue, and started sucking Felicia titties nipples one by one.....

I can't believe I got a dick in my pussy, a dick in my mouth, and another woman sucking my titties all at the same time, Felicia thought to herself.

Felicia kept cumming back to back hoping that all three wouldn't ever stop.....

Felicia opened her eyes looking up at Chad, as she felt Chads dick getting harder she knew he was getting ready to nut so she took his dick out of her mouth and begged him to nut in her face, and he nutted in her mouth and face.....

Mike laid Felicia on the couch on her back wanting more of that pussy he held her legs in the air and started stuffing his dick in and out of it.....

"Get on all fours on the floor," Chad told Rita.....

Chad stuffed his dick in Rita hard and fast as if he was made at the world, and she loved it. Chad worked the pussy, while she played with her own pearl tongue desiring to cum quicker and more pleasurable, and she did a great job of it.....

Chad told Rita to lie on her back on the floor, as his commence to tonguing and sucking her pussy. Mike stop fucking Felicia to eat Rita's pussy after Chad. Then Felicia ate Rita's pussy after Mike.....

Mike laid on the floor and both girls started sucking his dick at the same time, as Chad started taking turns fucking both girls from the back.....

As Mike nut came out he let it go in Felicia face and mouth. Then the girls started kissing each other as Chad continued stuffing his dick in and out of Felicia's pussy.....

After sex that night they showered and Mike drove Felicia home.....

After that night Chad and Rita did foursomes with Mike and Felicia, and sometimes threesomes with Felicia, and sometimes threesomes with just Mike.....

About nine months after that night Felicia, and Mike got married, and their marriage turned out to be a happy one.....

"Loco this book is a bomb fam," Twon said. "I knew you'd like it that's why I gave it to you, reading a good book takes your mind off bullshit," Loco said. "I only read chapter one, but it was hot, I couldn't stop reading it," Twon said. "I know that's why I gave it to you. I got a gang of books for you to read. I only read erotica when I'm alone. I mainly read nonfiction, and spiritual guidance books. I'm finna go to sleep so I want to cut the light off man, so can you wait to tomorrow to do some more reading," Loco said. "Yeah I'm cool on the light, you can cut it off," Twon said.

Twon laid back on the top bunk with constant visions of Rita, and Felicia having threesome with him. Twon dick stayed hard for hours, it was like he had popped some Viagra or something.....

CHAPTER 2

A few days later they were let off lock down Twon was able to get through to his family; they were happy to hear from him and disappointed that he was locked up for a murder. They immediately start sending money orders and religious pamphlets amongst other things. They were anxious for visiting day to come so they could come see him.....

Once visiting day came Twon, and everybody on the deck was preparing for visiting day.

Twon got quite a few visits from family members and friends showing love and support. They all promised that they'll always be there through the trials and tribulations of his case.

At the end of the day Twon last visitor showed up; it was his four month old pregnant girlfriend.....

Tears ran down her face in the visiting room as she cried out to Twon because she needed him there for support, and she knew that Twon wouldn't be there when the baby was born.

Twon left the visit early sad and confused knowing he wouldn't be there when the baby was born.....

Once he made it on the deck Loco could look at him and see and feel the sadness.....

Shortly after Twon's last visit they C/O's yelled out, "lock up time."

Once Twon and Loco made it within their cells Loco begin fixing burritos.....

"You think we should hook up all meat burritos, or this pasta I saved from dinner," Loco asked? "It don't matter," Twon said. "What's wrong, why you looking all sad for," Loco asked? "My girl on visits crying, talking about she can't do it without me, and that my baby gone be born without his daddy there, everything she said was the truth, sometimes the truth hurt, and it really hurted," Twon said. "Man, you got a body you might be fighting for two or three years, and then get found guilty, and gotta work on appeals. I understand how you feel because I got kids to, but you got a body man you gotta get with program. I know I aint gone never see the streets again I got to many cases, my rapy turned states, and I done caught gang of cases since I been in here and I might catch some more. But I don't let shit get me down I keep my head up to the sky, and just keep, keeping on. I must admit I aint been to church in a long time but I do pray to God; what you need to do is pray, theirs power in prayer," Loco said. "I got to do some reading tonight. How long you gone be with them burritos," Twon asked? "Be patient they'll be ready in no time, let the young chef work his magic," Loco said, as they both begin laughing.....

"Damn these burritos is a bomb, what you put on them some Mexican dip or some shit," Twon said as they begin laughing. "Naw that some homemade bar-b-que sauce," Loco said. "Whatever it is it's a bomb," Twon said.....

I wonder what I'm going to read tonight. I can't read no sex stories while Loco in the cell with me them sex stories to hot, Twon thought to his self as he continued eating his burrito....

Loco reached under his bunk and went in his brown paper bag filled with books, and pulled out a book that was average size in length but small width. The book was only a hundred pages. He handt the book to Twon.....

"What kind of book is this," Twon asked as he reached for the book. "This a book poetry, it aint regular poetry it's called ghetto poetry it's kind of like handwritten rap mixed with hardcore open mic poetry, you'll like it trust," Loco said.

Twon looked at the cover of the book, it looked like the cover of a rap C.D. He seen this little short big head bald head dude, with a black, and gray fur vest on the cover, which was the author. He read the title ghetto poetry by Flame.

"What kind of name is Flame," Twon asked? "It's not his real name, some authors use a pen name just like how rappers use different names, some authors do the same," Loco said. "I don't want to read no poetry," Twon said as he tried to hand him the book back. "Read it you'll like, remember when I gave you the sex stories you was acting the same way, then when you start reading it you feel in love," Loco said.....

Twon didn't respond but instantly got on the top bunk, and began reading the book. He skipped through the acknowledgements and went straight to the first page and began reading:

1
New

On the new investigated to see if black and gold or black and blue.
Visions never knew the goodness of the truth.
We were self-made kings, and queens, and humanized gurus.
Never knew it was designed for the black beauties to improve.
Lost and confused a minute issue was overdue.
Stabbed up a hundred something times, by his own multitude.
A fool sacrifice his own life, tossed away like rotten fruit.....
He never knew, never growed, never grew.

That poem was descent, Twon thought to himself, as he decided to read more:

2
Friends

Friends that was once friends changed on me in the end. Literally murdered
my uncle, my next of kin, while I resided in the belly of the beast within.
To his killer they be-friend.
In God we trust, not men.
Fake tears at funeral, basement tattoos on skin.
Open up on his joint claimed it as their own land.
Sexed his girlfriend.
Once I was released they walked up to me to shake my hand as nothing never
happen.
In the beginning and the end problems occurred through my so called friends.

3
A Way To Live A Way To Die

Pitiful Cries.
Whip away tears from eyes.
Knowing that it's heaven above the skies when we die.
First you must be baptized, free from all sinful ties, be a product of Godly
things in others eyes.
Speak the truth not a lie.
Use scriptures to abide by the Lords guide, and as a way to survive.
Worship God until you die.

4
Love and Hate

It's a thin line between love and hate.
Be careful, watch for chameleon of snakes, even your homies, and ones you
date.
Demons that made the creator close heavens gates, enemy of the states.
Control fate.
Be careful not to cross that thin line between love and hate where firely
sparks have already set a date, sealed fate.
Kill and take.
Love and hate.

5
She Wanted To Fly

She said she wanted to soar like a bald eagle, so high.

I asked her how high.

She said she wanted to reach the sky.

She really believe she could fly, she literally wanted to touch the sky one day before she die.

She sat by looking out her project window smoking a dip cigarette to get high

with no hesitation jumped out of the window saying, "I can fly, I can fly, I

can fly," right before her skull hit the ground cracking open a thousand times.

She wanted to fly a suicidal way to die.

Could never be forgiving for that suicidal sin she had to try, no heaven in

the sky.

Her soul shall forever burn in eternal fire.

Right before she die, she wanted to fly.

"Loco, these ghetto poems cool, who put you up on these," Twon asked? "A lot of people know about Flame he from the streets, I heard the nigga did fifteen straight for attempt murders. The niggas that use to work for him fucked up some money, and he fucked them up, and they got down on him in court. While he was in jail he wrote a gang of books then he got out, he got them published and got rich," Loco said. "Straight up?" "Yep. I heard he was one of them Travelers from off California, and Flournoy," Loco said. "Aw yeah," Twon said. "How long you gone be with the light man, I'm about ready to go to sleep," Loco said. "I wanna finish reading this book it won't take long. Soon as I get finished I'll cut the light off," Twon said. "Hurry up, nigga," Loco said, as he laid on the bottom bunk putting the blanket over his head.....

Twon continued to read the book, it seemed as each individual poem got even better each time he flipped to another page.....

In no time Twon finished the book hit the light, and laid on his bunk. It was hard for Twon to go straight to sleep because they were hollering out the doors for hours. He couldn't wait until they shut the fuck up.....

The next day the deck went up Loco stabbed a nigga in his eye for making that noise while he was trying to sleep the night before in return Loco was stabbed five times in the back, Twon got stabbed once in the hand, and others from both side the fin and the six got fucked up real bad.....

Loco was sent to the outside hospital .Once released from the hospital he was sent to seg with Twon amongst a bunch of others, some had went to the health care part of the county jail. Loco caught a new case which was nothing to him.

Twon and Loco stayed in seg. For thirty days. When they got out they were placed on the same deck, but not the same cell.....

This time Twon was smart he found a way to get a hold to some knives for security purposes. The ViceLords on that deck had plenty knives but he wanted his own for protection......

The next day after Twon was released from seg. it was Twon's first court date. He went and met his public defender for the first time.

His public defender was an African he hadn't look over any of Twons evidence yet, but scheduled the next court date to the next month.....

Twon made it to the deck, and his celly was on a special out of town visit, so Twon decided to ease his mind by reading a sex story.....

Twon begin reading this erotica book called Sexy Love, it was a book he got from Loco the day before..... Chapter 1

Starving Artist

Here I was a twenty seven year old starving artist.....

All through high school I tried to figure out what I'd major in when start college. Well it wasn't anything that I'd like to build a career in; until my senior year in high school.

In my senior year of high school I begin to visit art galleries with one of my friends and I really begin to take a liking in art.....

I started to read stories about ancient artist. One of the main things I liked about some of the artist, that they would paint portraits that wouldn't look like anything in particular, and they wouldn't make any sense to the eyes of the beholder, but the public still loved them.

After I graduated high school I decided to take art classes that taught students the very essence of painting artwork. I had already been doing drawings since I was a kid, therefore the classes were easy for me.

After I completed the art classes I decided to move out of my moms and dads home to a apartment on the other side of town.

I first started doing paintings of average things like cartoon characters, the president, and celebrities which sold a little through my Facebook page, and some viewers would come to my apartment to buy paintings.

My family and friends started asking me to do personal paintings of them and their family. Other people would see those paintings, and come through for personal paintings as well. But the money I was making still wasn't sufficient to sustain all my bills by myself.....

One light night I'm searching through my e-mails, one lady had e-mailed me asking if I could paint nude photos of her. Hell yeah, I thought to myself.

I e-mailed her saying yes, she e-mailed me right back asking the time, and place. I mentioned to her that it would be best if she could come over to my apartment the next night.

The next night came, and I awaited for her to come, she was a little late beyond our regularly scheduled time.....

I heard a knock at my door, I knew it was her because I wasn't expecting any other visitors. I looked through my peep hole, and seen this old lady standing there. Who is this old lady, this can't be the one requesting artwork of nudity, I thought to myself.

I opened the door she stuck her hand out to shake my hand, and said, "Hi, I'm Mary Ann I'm here to have the portrait painted of me." "My name is Steven, but you can just call me Steve, come on in," I said.

As she stepped in the door I begin checking this old lady out she was strap, she had a body better than most young women. She wore this beautiful full length black skirt with her cleavage showing with high heels on.....

She stepped in looking around admiring the artwork.....

"So where is the painting of the portrait going to take place," she asked when I became aware of her country accent. "Right here in the living room," I said. "Are we alone," she asked? "Of course," I said while looking directly in her beautiful blue eyes.....

She slowly undresses as if it was a strip tease, or as if we were getting ready to partake in the art of love making.....

I was stuck in a state of shock staring at this older lady beautiful body, as my cock got hard as concrete, I just wanted to give her vagina my cock in its entirety.....

"You must like what you see," she said. "I love what I see," I said.....

She laid down flat on her stomach with one of her finger slightly in her mouth, and told me this how she wanted me to paint the portrait.....

This old lady looked as if she was in her early forties, but looked wonderful, she was definitely someone I'd be interested in getting with.....

I started painting my first nude portrait as her, and I remained silent, it was as my cock refuse to get off hard, as I was on the verge of painting a masterpiece.....

Usually when I painted people it would be a problem, because people tend to move, she didn't move not one bit; which was strange that she could just lay there naked for hours.....

After the portrait was done I looked at it amazed and proud of myself.....

I told her it was finish she got up, and looked at it, and begin jumping up and down in joy. As her totties and butt cheeks jiggled as she jumped up, and down made my cock get even harder.

She paid me my money gave me a hug, and told me she will back tomorrow to get her painting once it's totally dry.....

All night long I dreamed of that lady's naked body.....

The next day she came and got her portrait, and told me she'd come back soon for me to paint more portraits', I gave my cell number so she wouldn't have to go through my e-mail or Facebook to get in touch with me.....

A week had went pass she called but I didn't recognize the number so I answered it, it was Mary Ann. She asked when could she come through to get more nude portraits done, I told her right now.

She came through, and I painted a portrait of her standing up naked.....

After that day she'd come every three days to get a nude portrait painting.....

I'm a human being, and heterosexual therefore I wanted to bang her more than you can imagine; but I didn't want to interrupt our business venture so I kept it professional.....

The fifth time she wanted me to paint a close up picture of just her vagina, I thought I was in heaven.....

After I finished painting her vagina she asked me to rub some baby oil on her. She laid flat on her stomach and told me to rub some baby oil on her back. As I begin rubbing it on her back she kept telling me to go down further once I got to the end of her back I told her I couldn't go down any further. She asked me why not I told her that I was at the end of her back. She asked me to rub some on her butt cheeks, I couldn't believe it. I started gently rubbing baby oil on her butt cheeks, my gently rubbing then turned to firm grips as she slightly moaned as if my cock was in her. I started to rub baby oil on her vagina as I gently slipped one, two, three, and then four fingers in and out of her, as she looked at me with the cutest sex face.....

I eagerly pulled my pants down hungry to give her my cock. Before I could stick it in she pleaded with me to give her my cock, and I did just that.....

When I first stuck my cock in her it felt wonderful it was tight, and moist it gripped my cock to perfection.....

I eagerly fed her vagina my all of my cock as hard and fast as I could as she begged me to stop because it was too much pain for her to handle.....

Once I was done she begin sucking in my cock without me even asking, and of course once she was done I returned the favor by eating her vagina.....

She spent a night over my house and we created pornography throughout the night on and off.....

Come to find out Mary Ann was fifty years old, and always wanted to show her body off to the the public, but never had the courage until I started painting those portraits of her.

After that night she placed my paintings of her in the nude on Facebook. Thanks to her my paintings sells were boosted. People from all over wanted me to do all sorts of paintings even those in the nude.

I never got the fame I wanted as an artist, as far as my paintings being in art galleries and shows. But I did get recognition from people that wanted personal paintings, and I made a lot of money off paintings.....

Maybe one day, possibly after I'm dead art galleries will exhibit my artwork.

As for me and Mary Ann she still comes over from time to time for me to do paintings of her in the nude, and for me to please her sexual lustful ways.....

Damn that was a bomb, Twon thought to his self as he begin looking for his bottle of lotion.....

CHAPTER 3

As time progressed along Twon became half use to and half tired of jail. The family and friends showed love, commissary, and visits every week.....

"What you doing man," Loco asked? "I'm getting ready for visits tomorrow," Twon said. "Aw yeah that's right visiting day is tomorrow," Loco said. "How in the hell did you get out your cell," Twon asked? "The police let me out to be the porter for tonight. I didn't wont shit I just stop by your cell to see what you was on, I'll let you finish shaving I'll see you tomorrow when the doors roll," Loco said. "A'ight," Twon said.....

Twon finished shaving, did a few push-ups, washed up in the sink, and went to sleep dreaming of the women he'd possibly see in the visiting room the next day.....

"Antwon Starks on that visit," the C/O said.....

Twon went to the visiting room, and to his surprise it was his pregnant ass girlfriend, she usually didn't come early in the morning.....

"What your pregnant ass doing coming up here to see me this early," Twon said. "I miss you," she said. "You just miss this big ass dick," Twon said. "Yeah I miss that to," she said. "I can't wait until you get out, it's just gone be me, you, and the baby," she said. "I aint even gone have time for you, I'm gone be with so many other ho's," Twon said. "Boy I wish you would. Why do you keep writing me them corny ass letters. How you gone be somebody daddy and you can't even spell grammar school words," she said as they both begin laughing.....

They stayed on visit for a while, both enjoyed seeing each other..... After the visit Twon went back to the deck and couldn't stop smiling.....

"Damn nigga you smiling hard, tell me what you so happy for, so I can be happy like you," Loco said. "Nothing much, when C/O's wasn't looking my girl pulled down her pants and showed me her pussy. I miss that pregnant pussy," Twon said. "I know you do, don't worry big dick Bob will take care the pussy for you," Loco said, as they begin laughing. "She talking about my letters is corny as hell," Twon said. "Yeah, you gotta learn to be raw with the pen that's how you survive in jail, I'll read one of your letters later or the next time you write," Loco said. "Imma write her tonight when we lock up, if you be the porter tonight I want you to come through and read it," Twon said. "Okay I got you, I gotta go make some calls," Loco said. "Yeah gotta try to get one of these phones myself to make sure my visits get to rolling through today," Twon said.....

All the rest of the day Twon got a lot of visits. Loco got a couple visits as well.....

"Play time is over you cowards lock it up," the C/O said.....

"Fam you finished writing the letter yet," Loco said. "Naw not yet we only been locked up for about ten or fifteen minutes, come back later right before the police lock you up in the cell," Twon said. "Okay, ten, four," Loco said.....

"It's been almost two hours, you told me to come back before lock up time, we getting ready to lock up in a lil while, where the letter at," Loco asked? "Here it go," Twon said, as he handt him the letter.....

Loco begin reading the letter.....

In no time flat Loco begin to laugh out loud, and then handt him the letter back.....

"Man is you serious, you can't write no letters like this to no ho's, you can't write no letter like this to nobody. You gotta learn to write letters that's how niggas survive in jail. A gotta go the police calling me to lock up. I'll holla at you in the morning," Loco said. "A'ight love my nigga," Twon said. "Love nigga," Loco replied.....

The next morning and days to follow Loco tried teaching Twon how to properly write letters. Twon just didn't get it. Twon barely made it through grammar school, and only went to high school for three weeks before dropping out.....

CHAPTER 4

It was time for court again, and Twon's public defender still hadn't looked over any of the evidence all he did was got him another continuous.....

After that day each time Twon went to court it was the same thing, continuous after continuous.....

On Twon's fourth courtdate to his surprise his P.D. had brought forth all the evidence the state had against him, which was one surveillance vides, and one eye witness. The eyewitness said she seen him walk Abdula in the store at gun point but couldn't totally make out his face because it was partially covered. The surveillance video showed everything that happen within the store, but didn't fully show Twon's face because it was partially covered.....

In reality the only reason he got booked is because the niggas that was with him went to the hood running off at the mouth.....

"So if the eyewitness, and the video didn't positively I.D. me, what am I doing in jail for than," Twon asked? "Because the eyewitness picked you out of a line up, which is not proper lawful procedure, because at first she said she couldn't positively I.D. you, then she said in the lineup she was positive it was you. All my years as a public defender I done seen all type of court cases similar to this one, and the defendant still got found guilty, and got a lot of time," the P.D. said. "So do you think you can beat it," Twon asked? "Of course I do, but like I just mentioned I done seen people get found guilty on all sorts of cases where the evidence was faulty. I got to go to another courtroom so I'll see you on the next court date," the P.D. said "Okay thanks man," Twon said.....

Twon went back to the deck smiling.....

"Fam what you smiling for you must got some good news, Loco said." Not really my P.D. told me that the eyewitness fucked up, at first she couldn't positively I.D. me, then when I went through the lineup she did positively I.D. me. And the P.D. said the surveillance video they got showed my face partially covered," Twon said. "Don't get me wrong I do hope, and pray you beat your case, but I done seen niggas get pinched for bogus murders a gang of times. But that's good you got some good news," Loco said. "I'm sleepy as hell Imma gone to my cell, and lay it down," Twon said.....

"Antwon Starks," the C/O said. "Celly wake up you got mail," Twon celly said. "Antwon Starks," the C/O said again. "Celly, celly wake up you got mail," Twon celly said again.....

Twon woke up out of his sleep got his mail, sat on his bunk reading the letter, and looking at the pictures that was in the envelope with the mail.....

When the doors rolled Twon ran straight to Loco's cell to show him the new pictures.....

"Damn fam these pictures hot, I can't even see the thong it look like she showing straight ass shots. She sent a lot of them she must like showing her body off," Loco said. "She is a freak she like doing all type off shit, she take it up the ass and everything. The bitch say the only time she can cum is when see sucking a nigga dick," Twon said. "For real," Loco said. "Yep, so you know her head game is awesome," Twon said.

"She talking about my letters is a joke to her," Twon said. "I been told you, you gone have to step your game up on writing letters, you been locked up to many months not to be raw on writing letters," Loco said.....

Later that day Loco tried to give Twon some more game on writing letters.....

CHAPTER 5

"**M**om how are you doing," Twon said over the phone. "I'm good, son your daughter looks just like you," Twon's momma said. "Daughter I don't got no kids," Twon said. "Your girlfriend had the baby," his momma said. "She did, when," Twon asked? "A few days ago," his mom said. "Make sure to bring the baby on visiting day," Twon said. "We might can't bring her the first visiting day, depending on the weather. We took a lot of pictures of her I sent them off yesterday," his momma said. "Mom, what's her name," Twon asked? "She came out looking like one of God's Angel so we named her Angel," his mom said. "Angel.....Angel that's nice name," Twon said.....

For a little while they talked over the phone mainly about the baby, and up coming family social events.....

Twon ran to tell Loco about Angel, Loco was happy as if it was actually his very own child being born.....

They celebrated by drinking homemade liquor, smoked a little weed, and cooked all meat burritos.....

Twon received the pictures of Angel a couple days later, he couldn't believe how much she looked like him.....

Visiting day came and went, he got a lot of visits but not one of his baby momma, nor his new born Angel.....

The next visiting day came and his baby momma, and his daughter Angel showed up. Seeing his new baby brought an overwhelming joy that he had never received in life. Once the visit was over he didn't even wanna leave the visitors room, but had no other choice.....

He promised his self that upon his release from prison he'd definitely be a good father to his daughter, unlike his father had been to him......

Throughout a year in the county Twon continue to get love, and support through family members, friends, his baby momma, and from other ho's.....

"Your last day of trial is today, blessings," Twon said to Loco. "I already know what it is I aint getting out of jail, but it is what it is," Loco said. "You gotta think positive," Twon said. "True that, but I'm a realist I'm not gone beat this body, and if I do I got to many cases I caught in jail, and I'll catch some more if a nigga want some trouble," Loco said. "I got faith that you gone beat your case tomorrow," Twon said. "I already know what it is," Loco said.....

The next Loco came in from court what a grin on his face.....

"I see you smiling so that's how I know you beat the case," Twon said.....

Loco begin laughing devilishly.....

"Naw I aint beat it all twelve people outta the jury found me guilty," Loco said. "So, why you smiling," Twon asked? "I just seen this thick ass new C/O down stairs," Loco said. "Man that's fucked up they found you guilty," Twon said. "I already knew they were, I just hope they don't give me the death penalty," Loco said.....

Twon got quiet started to think about his case, and how he'd feel if he got found guilty.....

"Don't tell nobody, nobody that I got found guilty," Loco said. "You know I aint gone say nothing. When you go back to get your time," Twon asked? "Next week, I'm finna lock up in the cell fall back, and do some reading, I'll holla at you later," Loco said.....

All day and the rest of the night Twon started to worry about his case more and more.....

The week to follow Loco came back from court and told Twon they gave him sixty years. Twon felt sorry for him. But Loco was happy that he didn't get a natural ball, or the death penalty, and his lawyer had filed his appeal.....

The week after that Loco was shipped off to the joint start his bide. When Loco left a piece Twon left with him. Loco was Twon right hand man, a true friend. Twon had other niggas he fucked with on the deck, and in the building, but he didn't fuck with them to the fullest degree like he had did Loco.....

Shortly after Loco left Twon's world seem to be falling apart: money orders and visits started to get slow. And even his baby momma started playing games; she even slowed down on bringing the baby to see him.....

Chapter Samples of previously
published book by Alan Hines

Queen of Queens

QUEEN OF
QUEENS

By

Alan Hines

PROLOGUE

I t was the summer of July 4th 1971, 11:30 P.M.,in Chicago as the fireworks lit up the skies.

CHAPTER 1

66 **Y**ou sure this the right spot man" Slim asked? "I'm positive this is the right spot, I wouldn't never bring you on no blank mission," Double J said.

With no hesitation Double J kicked in the door and yelled, "Police lay the fuck down".

Double J and Slim stormed in the crib with guns in hand ready to fuck a nigga up if anybody made any false moves.

As they entered the crib they immediately noticed two women sitting at the table;the women was getting ready to shake up some dope.

One of the women laid on the floor face down, crying out "please, please don't shoot me".....

She had seen many t.v. shows and movies in which the police kicked in doors and wrongfully thought an individual was strap or reaching for a gun when they wasn't, as the police hideously shot them taking their life line from em.

The other woman tried to run and jump outta the window; before she could do so Double J tackled her down and handcuffed her.

Double J threw Slim a pair of handcuffs, "handcuff her",Double J said. As Slim begin to handcuff the other chick he begin thinking to himself, were the fuck this nigga get some motherfucking handcuffs from.

The woman that was on the floor crying looked up and noticed that Slim wasn't the police.

"You niggas ain't no motherfucking police," she said. Double J ran over and kicked her in the face, and busted her nose.

"Bitch shut the fuck up",Double J said. She shut up, laid her head on the floor. As her head was filled with pain, while tears ran down her face, with blood running from her nose she silently prayed that this real life nightmare would come to an end!

Simultaneously Slim and Double J looked at the table filled with dope. Both Slim and Double J mouths drop;they'd never seen so much dope in their lives. Right in front of their eyes was 100 grams of pure uncut heroin.

Both women laid on the floor scared to death;they'd never been so scared in their natural lives.

Double J went into the kitchen found some zip lock bags, came back and put the dope in them, and then stuffed the dope in the sleeves of his jacket cause it was too much dope to fit in his pockets.

"Man we gotta hurry up, you know the neighbors probably heard us kick the door in," Slim said. "The neighbors ain't heard shit cuz of all the fireworks going off. That's why I picked this time to run off in here, while the fireworks going off so nobody won't hear us," Double J said. "Shiit they could've still heard us, the fireworks ain't going off inside the building," Slim said. "Don't worry about it," Double J said.

"Lord lets search the rooms before we leave, you know if all this dope is here it gotta be some guns or money in here somewhere," Double J said. "Yep, Jo I bet you it is," Slim said.

Double J walked over to the woman whom nose he busted kneeled to his knees put a .357 to her ear and clicked the hammer back.

The woman heard the hammer click in her ear, she became so scared that she literally shitted on herself.

"Bitch am a ask you one time, where the rest of that shit at," Double J asked in a deep hideous voice? She begin crying out and yelling, "it's in the closet in the bottom of the dirty cloths hamper."

Double J went into the closet snatched all the cloths outta the hamper and found ten big bundles of money. He seen a book bag hanging in the closet, grabbed it and loaded the money in it.

Double J went back into the front room, without second guessing it he shot both women in the back of their heads two times a piece.

Double J and Slim fled from the apartment building, got into their steamer and smashed off.

As Double J drove a few blocks away Slim sat in the passenger side of the car looking over at Double J pissed off.

"Lord, why the fuck you shoot them ho's," Slim asked with hostility? "Look at all the money and dope we got," Double J said. "What that gotta do with it," Slim asked? "You know that, that wasn't them ho's shit, they was working for some nigga, and if that nigga ever found out we stuck him up for all that shit he'd have a price on our heads. Now that the only people who knew about us taking that shit is dead we don't gotta worry about that shit," Double J said. Yeah you right about that, Slim thought to himself as he remained silent for a few seconds.....

"You just said something about dope and money, what money," Slim asked? "Look in the book bag," Double J said.

Slim unzipped the book bag and it was as he'd seen a million dollars. His mouth dropped, amazed by all the money that was in the book bag.

They hit the e-way and set fire to a lace joint as they begun to think of all of the things they'd be able to do with the money and dope.....

Double J and Slim were two petty hustlers looking for this one big lick, and they finally got it.

They had various hustles that consist of robbing, car theiving, and selling a little dope. All their hustles revovled around King Phill. King Phill was a king of a branch of ViceLords, the(I.V.L.) Insane Vice Lords. They'd rob, steal cars, and sell dope through King Phill, one way or the other.

Double J and Slim were basically King Phill's yes men. Whatever Phill would say or wanted them to do they'd say yes to.

After 45 minutes of driving they parked the steamer on a deserted block where there was no houses, only a big empty park.

Double J begin wiping off the inside of the car. Slim begin to do the same.

"Make sure you wipe off everything real good, we don't wanna leave no fingerprints," Double J said. "You aint gotta tell me, that's the last thing I wanna do is get pinched for a pussy ass stick up murder," Slim said.

Double J put the book bag on his back and they left the car wiping off the inside and outside door handles and they begin walking to Double J's crib, which was about thirty minutes away.

"Lord fire up one of them lace joints," Slim said. "Here you fire it up," Double J said as he passed the joint to Slim. Slim instantly set fire to it. They walked swiftly to Double J's crib, continuously puffing on the lace joints.

Once they made it halfway there, out of nowhere, Double J stopped in his tracks.

"What the fuck you stop for," Slim asked? "Lord we gotta get rid of that car," Double J said. "Why," Slim asked? "Cuz, like you said we don't wanna get pinched for no stick up murder. If somebody seen that car leave the scene of the crime and they tell the police and the police find the car and dust it for fingerprints, and find one fingerprint that matches one of ours we booked. We'll be sitting on death row saying what we should've, would've, and could've done," Double J said. "How we gone get rid of it," Slim asked?

"Here take my gun and bookbag, and meet me at my crib, my girl there she'll let you in," Double J said.

"You still didn't answer my question," Slim said. "What's that," Double J asked? "How we gone get rid of the car," Slim asked? "Don't worry about it, I got it," Double J said. "Let's get rid of it together," Slim said. "Naw man we need to make sure the money and dope is safe, and we need to get these hot ass guns off the streets," Double J said. "Where is the dope," Slim asked?

Double J reached in his sleeves pulled out the dope and handed it all to Slim as they departed and went their separate ways.....

I hope this nigga don't get caught fucking around with that car, Slim thought to himself.

Double J went back to the car looking for something to use to set it on fire with.

He ended up finding some charcoal fluid in the trunk of the car, squeezed all the fluid out of the bottle all over the car, struck a match and threw it on the car as it instantly begin burning.

Double J took off running. He ran halfway home, and walked the other half.

Once Double J made it home, before he could even knock on the door or ring the doorbell Slim opened the door. Double J rushed in nervously and slammed the door behind himself and frantically locked it.

"Nigga what the fuck took you so long," Slim asked? "What took me so long, shiiit I ran halfway back, but anyway I took care of the business, I burned the car up," Double J said.

"How much dough we got," Double J asked? "I don't know I ain't even open the book bag up, I was waiting to you get here," Slim said. "See thats why I fuck with you, anybody else would've played me for some of the money and dope," Double J said. "You my nigga I would'nt never try to get over on you. To keep it real, you didn't even have to take me on the lick with you," Slim said.....

They went into the bathroom, locked the door and begin counting the money. Each bundle of money was a G.

"Damn lord we got 10 stacks and all this dope," Slim said.

"How we gone get rid of all this dope," Double J asked? "We gone sell it in grams," Slim said. "Naw man we need to sell it in bags, we'll make more money selling it in bags. The only problem is where we gone sell it at, you know anywhere we try to open up at they gone close us down," Double J said. "We gone sell it in the hood," Slim said. "Stop playing you know damn well we dead in the hood. You know if we open up in the hood they gone close us straight down," Double J Said. "We gone have to go through Phill," Slim said. "Yeah we'll get up with Phill tomorrow," Double J said.

"Man don't tell nobody where we got the dope from," Double J said. "Nigga, do I look like a lame to you? What the fuck I look like telling somebody about what we did," Slim said.

"I'm finna go to sleep, you might as well spend a night," Double J said. "Yeah I might as well spend a night," Slim said." I'll holla at you in the morning, I'm sleepy as hell," Double J said as he started to yawn. As Slim went and laid on the couch in the living room. Double J went into his bedroom undressed down to his boxers and t-shirt and got into bed with his wife who he assumed was asleep.

As Double J pulled the covers back he noticed that his wife was in bed asshole naked.

I'm glad I married her, Double J thought to himself while enjoying the view.....

Slim and Double J stayed awoke for a little while thinking about the money they had and the profit they was going to make off the dope.....

As Double J closed his eyes to go to sleep he felt his wife's hands gently slipping into his boxers rubbing on his dick.

"I thought you were asleep," Double J said." I ain't sleep, I was just laying here thinking about you," she said.

She continued rubbing on his dick.

"Now you know you can't be rubbing on my dick without any lubrication. That shit don't feel good when you do it with dry hands," Double J said.

She got up and squeezed a little Jergens in the palm of her hand, as he slipped his boxers off and laid back on the bed.

She grabbed his dick firmly, begin lathering it up with the lotion and jagging him off at the same time.

As she thoroughly jagged him off he pumped her hand until his nut unleashed on her titties, as she begin rubbing the nut around on her titties as if it was baby oil or lotion.

She then took his dick into her mouth gobbling it and the lotion in all swirling her tongue around it and sucking on it as if she was trying to suck some sweet nectar out of it.

Once it got rock hard she begin deep throating it, choking herself with his dick while rubbing on her own clitoris roughly while humming.

In no time flat he was releasing a load of nut down her throat.

She stood up, wiped her mouth and slightly begin growling she then got on top of him and played with his dick for a few seconds until it got back hard.

She looked him in his eyes, as she grabbed his dick firmly and shoved it in her pussy, and begin smiling.....

She begin riding it slowly to get her pussy totally wet, as he grabbed her ass cheeks guiding her movements.

Once her pussy got wet he begin slamming his dick in and out of her, enjoying the tightness of her moist pussy. As she clawed his chest moaning in the midst of pleasure and pain;she liked when it hurted.

It felt so good to him that every time he'd slam his dick up in her pussy it felt like he was actually nutting each time.

As Double J begin to nut, she was cumming simultaneously as he begin to slam his dick in and out her pussy rougher and harder, she begin fucking him back;it was like a rodeo show as their orgasms exploded.

"Get up, get on the bed so I can hit it from the back," Double J said. She got on all fours on the bed.

Double J got on his knees right behind her and began squeezing and rubbing her big brown pretty ass cheeks.

"Tell me you love me before you start fucking me," she said. "I love your hot ass," he said.

Double J then rammed his dick in her hot pussy gripping her ass cheeks and slamming his dick in and out her pussy hard and fast while admiring the way her ass cheeks bounced.

In no time he was letting another nut explode in her pussy.

"Let me suck it," she said in a low seductive tone. "Hold on let me roll up a joint," Double J said. "You know that I don't like the smell of lace joints, why you got to lace your weed with cocaine? Why you can't smoke regular weed like everybody else," she said.

Double J begin smiling, and looking her straight in the eyes.

"We'll I'll smoke a regular joint just for you," Double J said.

He rolled up a regular joint with only weed in it. Set fire to it as she got on her knees with an aim to please.

As he inhaled and exhaled the potent weed smoke she simultaneously sucked his dick utilizing a suction method sucking mainly the tip thoroughly.

From the potent effect of the weed, combined with her superb suction method, and the moisture of her mouth felt so good that within seconds he released a glob of nut in her face.

He finished smoking his joint and both of them laid on the bed.

"You must really been wanting to fuck?," Double J asked. "I been thinking about you all day at work. I had to take off work because I creamed in my panties daydreaming about your dick going in and out my pussy and mouth. I been sitting in the house all day waiting on you," she said.

I done married a freak, Double J thought to himself.

They begin to tell each other how much they loved one another. And how their lives wouldn't be the same without each other, before both of them fell into a deep sleep.....

The next morning after Double J's wife had went to work Double J and Slim sat at the kitchen table eating breakfast, reminiscing about the stick up and the murders.

They glorified and celebrated the stick up and the murders as if they were professional athletes that just won a championship game, or as if they had won the lottery.

It's sad how bloodshed make others glad. But this life some live as thugs consist of no love.

Other people were brought up to increase the peace and strive to earn college degrees, and live the American dream.

But those that live the street life thrive on death and destruction;they rob, steal, and kill with no discretion, and glorify others name that do the same.....

"Hurry up and finish eating so we can go holla at Phill," Double J said. "I'm already finished," Slim said. "Well empty the rest of that shit that's on the plate in the garbage and put that plate in the sink," Double J said.

Slim emptied the rest of the food in the garbage and put the plate in the sink, and went and grabbed the book bag.

"Naw we gone leave the dope and shit here unless you wanna take your half to your house," Double J said. "It's cool, I'll leave it here," Slim said.

As they rode up the block in the hood where Phill was they noticed many of the Insanes on Phill's security as usual.

Once they made it to where Phill was, Phill began smiling cuz he was happy to see them he needed them to take care of some business for him.

King Phill was a pretty boy. Stood about 6'5 half latino, half black with naturally curly black hair in his mid twenties.

For those that didn't know Phill personally that would've never believed that he was a king of a large street gang. King Phill looked like a pretty boy college student.....

"Park the car I need to holla at ya'll," Phill said.

They parked and got out to holla at him.

"I need ya'll to get some steamers for me," Phill said. "We ain't on no car thieving shit right now, we need your assistance on some other shit," Double J said. "What ya'll need?" Phill asked.

"Let's step away from everybody it's personal," Slim said.

As they stepped away from everybody else Phill begin trying to figure out what Double J, and Slim wanted. Maybe they finna ask for some shit Phill thought to himself.

"Phill we got some dope we need to get it off," Double J said. "What you talking about," Phill asked? "We need to pop it off in the hood," Slim said. "What ya'll talking about opening up a dope spot in the hood," Phill asked? "That's exactly what we're talking about," Slim said. "You know ya'll can't work in the hood if ya'll ain't a 5 star universal elite," Phill said. "I told him," Double J said. "Well make us universal elites," Slim said.

Phill begin laughing.....

"I don't just give out status like that, I ain't one of these phony ass nigga's that let people buy status, you gotta earn it fucking with me," Phill said.

Slim looked at Phill like he was crazy.....

"Earn it, all the shit we do for you, and for the hood. While them niggas you made universal elites be in the Bahamas some motherfucking where, we be doing all the shootings for the hood, and all type of other shit for you and the hood," Slim said. "Yeah you do got a point, cuz ya'll do stand on nation business. This what I'm going to do for ya'll. Am a let ya'll work in the hood under my name, but ya'll gotta pay," Phill said. "How much we gotta pay," Slim asked? "That depends on how much dope ya'll got," Phill said. "We got ten grams," Double J said..... He was lying. "Ten grams that ain't shit. Ya'll work them ten grams for two or three weeks outta Argale park. In two or three weeks ya'll should've atleast double or tripled them ten grams. Once ya'll do ya'll gotta give me a stack every week," Phill said.....

Double J and Slim looked at each other smiling knowing it was finna be on.

"A stack a week we got you," Double J said.

"We'll holla at you, I gotta go pick my girl up from work," Double J said..... He was lying.....

As Double J and Slim got into the car and rode off listening to Al Green's Love and Happiness they were happier than a kid on Christmas Day.....

CHAPTER 2

Three Days Later

"How much is that small black digital scale," Double J asked the cashier? "That one right there is a hundred dollars. But I'd recommend this white one right here if you're going to be weighing things over twenty eight grams. Alot of customers usually buy that small black one, then later on down the line the same customers come back and buy a bigger one, which is a waste of money to me," the woman cashier said. "How much do the white one cost," Slim asked? "Two hundred," the cashier said. "We'll take it," Slim said. "Will that be it," the cashier asked? "Naw we need five bottles of dorms, and a bundle of them little black baggies right there, and two of them mac spoons," Slim said.....

As other customers walked into small record store the cashier paused and begun covering up the small area where contraband was being sold.

"Thomas, can you service the new customers," the female cashier said to her co-worker.....

"Wait til these customers leave, then I'll give ya'll, ya'll items," the female cashier said to Double J and Slim.....

"Ya'll sell scales, baggies, and all type of shit to everybody in the city, and now you wanna act like it's top secret," Slim said. "Yeah we do supply alot of people with contraband, but those are only the people that come in here asking for it. We can't have contraband on display because it's all type of people that come in here. A person might come in here with their kids. Or an off duty police officer might come in here to buy some records. And if they see all of this contraband on display they'll report our ass to the city. We won't loose our store or anything like that, but we'll have to pay a healthy fine," the cashier said.....

Within minutes the other customers purchased their records and left the store.....

"Your total will come out to $375.00," she said.....

Slim paid her and they left the store.....

Once they made it to Double J's crib they immediately weighed the dope for the first time.....

"Damn lord we got a hundred grams, I thought it'll be about fifty grams," Slim said. "Yeah me to," Double J said. "Aw we finna put up numbers if this shit is a bomb," Slim said. "Showl is," Double J said.

"Why did you buy baggies instead of aluminum foil," Double J asked? "Cuz we gone put the dope in the baggies, we don't need no aluminum foil," Slim said. "But we need to put it in the aluminum foil so it can stay fresh," Double J said. "Once we put it in the baggies, then put some thick clear tape on the baggies the dope will stay fresh," Slim said.

"We need to find us a connect on some quinine," Double J said. "Naw we aint gone put no quinine or none of that other crazy shit on the dope. We either gone use dorms or sell it with no mix on it at all," Slim said.

"We gone put three pills on each gram of dope," Slim said.

"How many grams we gone bag up the first time," Double J asked? "We gone bag up ten grams first and put it out there and see what it do, you know we can't bag up to much cuz if it don't sell quick enough it'll fall off," Slim said. "That's my point exactly, that's why I ask," Double J said.

Double J weighed out ten grams on the scale. Then Double J and Slim opened up thirty dorms which was actually capsules. Double J and Slim then grabbed two playing cards a piece and begin mixing the dope with the dorms.....

"How many mac spoons we gone use," Double J asked? "We gone give up two macs for a sawbuck and see how that go first. I'f the dope is a bomb we gone drop down to one mac spoon or a mac and a half. That all depends on how good the dope is. And if it's real good we gone put more dorms on it," Slim said.

Double J and Slim grabbed a mac spoon a piece and begin measuring the dope, and putting it in the bags.....

"I got some thick clear tape in my room in the closet," Double J said. "Wait to we get finished before you go get it," Slim said.....

After about an hour and a half they'd finally finished bagging up the dope.....

"Let's count it up to see how much we bagged up," Double J said.

"We gone put twelve blows in a pack, whoever sell the pack get twenty dollars, and turn us in a hundred," Slim said. "How much we gone pay people to run the joint," Double J asked? "We ain't worried about that right now we gone run the joint ourselves. Once it pick up then we'll put people in play to run the joint. We'll worry about what we gone pay them when that time come," Slim said.....

As they sat at the table counting up the dope Slim begin to wonder who was they gone get to work the packs.....

"Shiiit who we gone get to work the joint," Slim asked? "My lil cousins gone work the joint. They been sweating me for the last couple days about when we gone open up the joint, so they can work. They juvenilles, so if they catch a case they momma's can just sign them out from the police station," Double J said.....

Once they finished counting the dope up it came out to twenty packs, and seven odds. They bagged up $2,070 not including the two blows in each pack for the pack workers to get paid.....

Slim begin doing the mathematics in his head.....

"So if we got two stacks off ten grams then we gone get atleast twenty stacks off of the whole hundred grams," Slim said. "Shiit we gone get more than that if the dope is a bomb, and if it can take more than three pills a gram," Double J said. "Yep showl is," Slim said.

"Go grab the tape outta the closet," Slim said.....

When he came back with the tape Slim examined it.....

"Yeah joe this tape perfect," Slim said.....

They put twelve bags on a strip of tape, then put another strip of tape over the bags.

They put the tape over the bags in order for the dope to stay fresh, and so none of the workers wouldn't dip in the bags.....

Double J and Slim grabbed the dope and a .45 automatic and went to pick up Double J's cousins, and set up shop in Argale Park.....

They posted up and the corners and in the park.

One of Double J's cousin walked through the hood telling all the dope fiends that they were passing out free dope in Argale Park. They dopefiends rushed to the park and spreaded the word.....

The two niggas that stood in the park, Double J's cousin was the ones passing out the samples to the dopefiends.....

A couple hours later the park was filled with dopefiends shopping for dope.

Double J and Slim couldn't believe how fast, and how many dopefiends were coming to buy dope.

Judging by the large amount of dopefiends that were coming to buy dope, so soon, Double J and Slim knew they had some good dope.

"Damn lord look how many dopefiends waiting in line to shop," Slim said. "That's cuz the dopefiends that we gave samples to went and told everybody that we got good dope, word of mouth travel," Double J said.

Within two days and one night Double J and Slim sold the whole hundred grams.....

"Lord who we gone buy some more dope from," Slim asked? "That's a good question," Double J said.

As they continue to smoke and ride through the hood they remained silent trying to figure out who they'd start buying weight on the dope from.

"We gone have to start buying from Phill," Double J said. "Phill got good dope but it aint a bomb," Slim said. "How you know, you don't even use dope," Double J said. "I can tell from the numbers his dope spots put up. His spots put up a little numbers but they aint all that," Slim said. "Who else we gone buy dope from, we gone have to get it from Phill," Double J said.....

"Ride through Lexington and see if he out there," Slim said.....

As they made it on Lexington they seen Phill standing on the corner with a gang of niggas standing around him on his security.....

"A Phill check it out Lord," Slim said.....

Phill walked towards them smiling.....

"Where's my money at," Phill said. "What money," Slim asked? "My g, what else money. I heard ya'll been tipping outta the park," Phill said. "We'll get the money we owe you a little later on," Slim said. "It aint even been a whole week," Double J said. "So what I want my money, ya'll been tipping," Phill said. "Aigh't we got you," Double J said.

"How much you'll sell us twenty five grams of dope for," Slim asked? "Three thousand," Phill said. "That's kinda high aint it," Double J said. "Naw that's low, anybody else I charge one fifty a gram. I'm only charging ya'll like one twenty five a gram, at one twenty five a gram twenty five grams suppose to come out to thirty one twenty five, but I just said a even three stacks, I aint tripping over a hundred and twenty five dollars. Look right I got shit I gotta do, is ya'll gone need that twenty five grams or not," Phill asked? "Yeah we need it now," Double J said. "I can't get it for ya'll right now but I'll have somebody get it for ya'll later," Phill said.

"We gone have the g we owe you to when you sell us the twenty five grams, so we'll bring the whole four thousand with us," Slim said.

"I gotta go, I'll holla at ya'll later on," Phill said. "Make sure we get them twenty five grams today our joint is outta work," Slim said. "I got ya'll don't worry about it," Phill said. "A'ight we'll holla at you," Slim said.....

Later on that day they were sitting in Double J's crib chilling, when they got a call from Phill telling them that he was going to send his guy John over with the twenty five grams, and that they needed to make sure the four stacks was counted up right before they gave it to John.....

Once John delivered the twenty five grams they went straight to Doubles J's kitchen table and started bagging up.....

"How many pills we gone use," Double J asked? "We gone use three first to see how the dopefiends like it with three on it," Slim said.....

Both of them begin opening up the seventy five capsules and dumping the inside of the dorms on the table on top of the twenty five grams.....

"Lord if this dope is any good we finna be getting money like never before. Fuck spending our money we need to stack our shit, and get into some real estate, then we can leave the dope game alone," Slim said. "Yeah I agree with you on that.

You know all these other niggas be spending their shit, then when it comes time for bound money they can't even bound out for ten or fifteen stacks," Double J said.....

As they continued mixing up the dope they both imagined of riches.....

They next day they put the dope on their joint, and to their surprise the dope fiends loved it.....

They finished that twenty five grams in one day, and was right back at Phill buying fifty grams this time. Phill was a player that liked to see niggas doing good getting money so he sold them fifty grams for fifty five hundred.....

Once they put that fifty grams out their they thought it would slow down some because the dopefiends would know from the last twenty five grams that they aint selling the same dope they had originally when they first opened up.....

Double J and Slim sat back at the end of the park admiring the veiw of the customers swarming to buy dope. It was as if everytime the pack worker would bring out a new pack the dopefiends would swarm on him like flies to shit.....

"How the hell is our joint tipping like this with Phill's dope, and his joint aint putting up numbers like ours," Double J asked? "That cuz Phill, and alot of these other niggas be putting that crazy shit on they dope, that's why I told you we aint gone use nothing but dorms. Phill nam still checking a bag but their turnover rate is slower," Slim said.....

Within a month Double J, and Slim was the men. Their joint was putting up numbers. They had bought new Cadillacs, new sports cars and all. Their team of workers constantly grew. Ho's coming from everywhere trying to get with them.....
Throughout it all they continued to buy dope from Phill.....

CHAPTER 3

One hot sunny day Double J was simply bending blocks in the hood listening to Al Green puffing on joints that wasn't laced with cocaine when he seen her from the back in those jeans.....

Damn this ho thick as hell, Double J thought to himself.

He pulled up to her; once he seen her face he became disappointed. Aw this Cynthia dopefiend ass, he thought to himself.

Cynthia immediately opened the passenger side door and just jumped in his car.....

"Take me to your spot to get some dope," she said. "I got a few bags in my pocket," Double J said. "What are you doing riding around with dope in your pocket," Cynthia asked? "What else am I doing with dope in my pocket," Double J said sarcastically. "I didn't know you shoot dope," Cynthia said. "Tell somebody, and I'll kill you," Double J said.

They drove to a quiet block on the outskirts of the hood, pulled over and parked.

Double J gave Cynthia the dope to hook it up and put in the needle.

Once she hooked the dope up and put it in the needle she tried handing the needle to Double J.

"Naw you go ahead, ladies first," Double J said.....

With her right hand she shot dope into the veins of her left arm as her eyes rolled in the back of her head, as her entire body felt as if it was taken to a whole nother planet.

Afterwards she passed the needle to Double J.

With his right hand he shot dope into the veins of his left arm.

As Barry White song I'm never gone leave your love played on the radio Double J felt as if he was soaring above the clouds.....

Afterwards Double J dropped Cynthia off at home and went and met Slim at his crib to shake up some dope.....

"I bought a hundred grams instead of fifty," Slim said. "That's cool," Double J said.

"Start busting the dorms down I gotta go use the bathroom, my stomach fucked up from smoking all them lace joints," Slim said.....

Slim came out the bathroom and seen Double J sitting at the table nodding and scratching.

"Damn nigga you look like you done had a dope," Slim said. "Naw man I'm just sleepy," Double J said.

So they both begin busting the dorms down.

Double J kept scratching and nodding at the table.

This nigga fucking around with dope, Slim thought to himself.

"Lord tell the truth aint you getting high," Slim asked? "Nigga you know damn well I been getting high ever since you've known me," Double J said. "Nigga you know what I'm talking about is you fucking with dope," Slim said.....

Double J paused for a little while.....

"Yeah I fuck around with the dope a little," Double J said. "What made you turn into a dopefiend," Double J asked? "I use to be seeing how dopefiends look after they get high. Some of them looked like it's the best feeling in the world. Some of them be looking like they're walking on the clouds or some shit. Then I start to see how the dopefiends do whatever it takes to get money for dope, that made me want to try some even more, cuz I knew it had to be some good shit. Once I tried it, it felt like heaven on Earth. No lie, am a be a dopefiend forever. Am a get high til I die," Double J said.

Slim looked at Double J with a smirk on his face thinking to himself, this nigga done lost his mind.....

"Niggas always trying to belittle dopefiends, when they get high they motherfucking self off all type of shit. A drug addict is a drug addict. It don't matter if you smoke weed, lace weed, tut cocaine, tut dope, or shoot dope you still a drug addict," Double J said. "I can agree with you on that cuz I smoke more lace joints than some people use dope," Slim said.

"We gone have to start paying somebody to bag up this dope this shit a headache," Slim said. "Straight up," Double J said.....

Days to follow Slim begin to admire how suave Double J was as he was high off dope.

As he walked, talked, drove, ate, smoke cigarettes, and each and every way he maneuvered was super cool when he was drunk off dope.....

Before long Slim begin asking Double J a gang of questions on how it feels to be high off dope.....

"You steady asking me about how it feels to be high off dope. My best answer is you wont know how it feels until you try it," Double J said. "I'm scared of needles," Slim said. "You aint gotta shot it, you can tut it. But it aint nothing look shooting it, as that dope run up your veins, it's the best high you'll ever experience," Double J said.

171

Slim was still hesitant to try dope he let his pride get in the way, he knew certain people looked down on dopefiends.....

A couple days later at a club with these two lesbian chicks he dated and paid for sex he begin wanting to try some dope again.

The lesbian chicks Tricey, and Reese did it all, besides dope. They snorted lines of cocaine, smoked lace joints, regular weed, and smoked leaf.....

After downing a few drinks at the club. The girls sat at the table snorting line after line of cocaine, secretly not in the publics eye.

"Damn ya'll gone fuck around and O.D.," Slim said. "That's only if you use dope, you ain't gonna find to many people O.Deing of cocaine, although you can O.D. off cocaine," Reese said.

"Have ya'll ever fucked around with dope before," Slim asked? "Hell naw, we aint no motherfucking dopefiends," Tricey said. "Shiiit ya'll get high off every thing else," Slim said. "Everything besides dope," Tricey said.

"I heard that dope is the best high known to mankind," Slim said. "Yeah me to. But it takes control over your body, you gotta have it or your body wont be able to function right. And I heard the sickness is a motherfucker," Tricey said.

"I wanna snort a line or two to see how it feels," Slim said. "So you wanna be a dopefiend," Reese said sarcastically. "Naw I just wanna snort just one bag of dope to see how it feels. I want ya'll to snort it with me," Slim said. "Hell naw," Reese said. "Let's all three of us try it together," Slim said.....

For almost an hour at the club Slim tried convincing the girls to snort a bag of dope with him, and it worked.....

Slim pulled up to his dope spot.....

"Tyrone who working Lord," Slim asked? "Ush working," Tyrone said. "Why don't I see nobody shopping," Slim asked? "It's kinda slow right now, but you can best believe it'll be a gang of customers in line in no time," Tyrone said.

"Go get me three bags of dope, and hurry up Lord," Slim said.

Tyrone rushed to go get three bags from Ush, and brought it right back to the car..... Slim took the dope and smashed off.

Slim parked a few blocks over from his joint.....

He tore open a bag of dope with his teeth and laid it on one of the girls cigarette box. He tore a piece of the paper off his match box. He scooped up half the dope and snorted it like a pro.

He sat the Newport box on the dash and leaned back in his seat to feel the total effect of the dope.

Within seconds Slim had his door opened bent over throwing up his guts.

I'f that shit gone have me throwing up like that I don't even want none, Tricey thought to herself.

After Slim finished throwing up he snorted the other half of the dope off of the Newport box.

He laid back in his seat and relaxed for minutes and begun to feel the effect of being drunk off dope.

The girls then snorted their bags.

As they laid there high they all thought within their own silent minds that dope was the best drug known to men.....

Slim, and both women winded up in a motel room. Slim dick stayed on hard all the while. Slim had heard of the dope dick, but didn't know that it was this intense.....

For the entire week to follow Slim snorted dope, and smoked laced joints each day.

One morning as Slim went home he got into it with his main girlfriend. She was tired of him spending nights out, and cheating on her..... She through some hot coffee on him, and swung on him a few times leaving him with a few minor scars on his face..... Slim stormed out the house and went to his joint.....

Slim pulled on the joint got two bags of dope pulled around the corner to blow them.....

He pulled back around to his joint sat on the hood of his car smoking a lace joint, thinking of all the good times, and the bad times he had, had with his girlfriend..... He was still a little pissed off cuz she put her hands on him.....

Double J pulled of laughing.....

"So I see you having problems with your girl," Double J said. "How you know," Slim asked? "Cuz I see you sitting there faced all scratched up looking crazy, I know you aint let no nigga do it to you, because we'll be in war right now," Double J said.....

Slim tossed the duck of the joint on the ground, and bailed in with Double J, and Double J pulled off.....

"Man this ho crazy as soon as I walked through the door she got to throwing shit, hollering, screaming, and swinging," Slim said. "We all go through problems with women, that's been going on since the beginning of time," Double J said.....

"Pull over for a minute I need to take care of some business," Slim said.

Double J pulled over and put the car in park.

"What you gotta piss or something," Double J asked? "Naw I need to take care of something else," Slim said.

Slim pulled out his pack of cigarettes. Then pulled out a bag of dope, opened it with his teeth and poured it on the cigarette box..... Double J remained silent couldn't believe what he was seeing.

Slim then pulled out a small piece of a straw and snorted the entire bag of dope. Double J just sat there looking at him like he was crazy.

Slim fired up a cigarette, and looked at Double J and asked, "Is my nose clean." "Yes it's clean," Double J said.

"I can't believe you sat there and snorted a bag of dope after you been getting down on me after you found out I was getting high," Double J said. "I been seeing how good you been looking when you high off dope, it be like you be walking on clouds or some shit, and I wanted that feeling so I tried it, and I love it,"

Slim said. "I told you it was a bomb, especially if you shoot it," Double J said.....

Double J begin smiling and pulled off listening to Barry White's song Ecstasy, as they drove to the mall.....

Once they made it inside the mall Slim became so happy with seeing all the ho's there that he had forgot all about what him and his girl had went through earlier.....

Slim winded up getting a gang of numbers from ho's.

As they entiered this one shoe store Slim couldn't take his eyes of this white chick. She was raw as hell. She was about 5.6", 140 Ibs., a red hed, with black eyeline around her red lipstick, with hazel blue eyes. She looked like a model or some shit.

Slim decided to walk over and strike up a conversation with her.....

Slim came to find out that her name was Angie, she lived on the north side of town. Twenty years of age with no boyfriend, no kids, or none of that. They exchanged numbers, and went their seperate ways.....

All the rest of the day Slim couldn't stop thinking of Angie she just looked so good to him.....

Slim went home that night, and made up with his girl, as they got down within break up to make up sex.....

Slim had never been with a white woman before but always wanted one..... The next day Slim winded up giving Angie a call, he thought she was gone be on some phony shit, but he was wrong she was real cool.....

Slim and Angie starting hanging out together damn near everyday..... One of the things Slim liked about Angie was that she genuinely liked him for him; she wasn't like the other women that he'd fucked around with, they was only interested in money one way or the other, Angie wasn't.....

Within a couple months Slim left his main girl for Angie, and moved in with her.....

Within several months Double J and Slim found there dope habits increasing. Having to spend more money to support their habits, for guns, money on bonding their guys outta jail, and started having to pay more bills. This fortune and fame wasn't all what it seemed.....

CHAPTER 4

"**R**oxanne you need a ride," Slim asked? "Naw no thank you, here come my bus now," Roxanne said. "Girl get in you aint gotta wait on no bus," Slim said. "No, it's okay, thanks anyway," Roxanne said. "Get in I insist," Slim said.....

She winded up getting in.....

She looked around the inside of his Cadillac and noticed that it was super clean. The upholstery looked as if it was brand new from the manufacturing place.....

He put on some Teddy Pendergrass, Turn off The Lights, as he pulled of she immediately made herself comfortable.

"Where do you need me to take you to," Slim asked? "I need you to drop me off at the Cook County hospital," she said. "Whats wrong with you," he asked? "Aint nothing wrong with me, I'm going to see my friend, she just had a baby," she said. "Do you have any kids," he asked? "I don't have no kids, nor a boyfriend," she said.....

Roxanne was one of Slims grammer school friends that he'd only see every once in a while..... On the rest of the short ride there they begin to reminisce about grammer school..... They both admitted that they had been liking each other since grammer school.....

As he pulled up in front of the hospital he tried to park.....

"Naw you aint gotta park. Just let me out in the front," she said. "You need me to come back and pick you up, when you get finished seeing your friend," he asked? "Naw I'm straight," she said. "What's up with later on let's go somewhere and fuck," Slim said as they both begin laughing. "Naw I'm just joking about fucking, but serious lets get together and kick it later on," he said.....

She reached into her purse and pulled out a little card with her phone number on it and handt it to him.....

"Well here go my number just call me later on tonight," she said.....

As she walked into the hospital Slim just sat there watching her in a daze imagining what she'd look like naked.....

Later on that day Slim called her as the phone rang seven times he didn't get any answer..... He called her three more times, periodically, but still didn't get no answer.

After calling her for the fifth time he finally got an answer.....

"Hello," she said. "Hello can I speak to Roxanne," Slim said. "Yes this is me," she said. "This Slim, let me come through and pick you up," he said. "Why you wait so late," she asked? "I been calling you all day, aint nobody answer the phone," he said. "I been running errands for my granny. I been in and out the house all day. You got bad timing, you must been calling the times when I was out. Fuck it come on over and pick me up we'll kick it for a little while," she said.....

He went over picked her up. They rode around seeing the sites and reminiscing for about thirty minutes. Then he took her back home.....

Days to follow he begin sneaking off from Angie to hang with Roxanne almost everyday for about two weeks straight. Each time they was together she refused to give the pussy up.....

One night Slim was drunk off dope, and liquor, and had been smoking lace joints. He had his mind set on fucking the shit outta Roxanne this particular night.

He went to her house unannounced. She got dressed and decided to kick it with him anyway.

As she entered his car she smelled the smoke from lace joints.....

"Why do you gotta smoke that stuff," she asked? "Cuz it makes me feel good, you need to try it," he said. "Never that, I'll never use drugs. I don't need drugs to make me feel good, I get high off life," she said. "Getting high off life, I liked that, that sounded slick," he said.

As they cruised down the street listening to Al Greens, Let's Stay Together, both of them became relaxed. She begin slowly taking off her shoes to get comfortable.

Outta the corner of his eyes he looked at her admiring her beauty.

"Let's go somewhere and chill out," he said. "We already chilling out," she said. "Naw let's get a room or something," he said. "Hell naw, we aint getting no room or none of that until you get rid of her, and let me become your main girl," she said. "Who is her," he asked? "You know who she is the woman that you go home to every night when you drop me off. The one you share your love and life with, the one you live with," she said.....

He paused trying to think of some good game to pop back at her but couldn't because he knew she was speaking the truth.....

"But I been with her for a long time now and I just can't up and leave her," he said. "Well whenever you do decide to leave her I'm willing to fill in her position and take on all responsibilities. And when I say all responsibilities thats exactly what I mean," she said as she looked him in his eyes seductively.....

As he cruise the streets they peacefully listened to Al Green as thoughts of her in pornographic positions raced through his mind he'd visualize his dick in and out her pussy, ass, and mouth.....

He pulled up at a liquor store and parked.....

"Do you want me to get you something to drink," he asked? "A pink lemonade," she said.

As he exited the car thoughts of him, and her walking down the aisle getting married raced through her mind.

She really liked him but the only way he was going to get between her legs was if she was his main girl and only girl.

He came back into the car with two bottles of Champagne, two cups, the pink lemonade, and a few bags of chips.

He instantly popped open a bottle and poured some Champagne in a cup. Handt her the other cup.

"Naw I'm straight you know I don't drink," she said. "Try it out just for tonight, just for me," he asked? "Thanks but no thanks, I don't drink," she said.

She grabbed the pink lemonade opened it and begin sipping on it like it was the best lemonade she ever had, as they pulled off and begun cruising through the town.....

Roxanne reached into her purse and pulled out a pickle. She took the pickle out of it's wrapper and begin sucking on it like it was a dick. For a long time she pulled the pickle in and out her mouth sucking on it like she was trying to suck out all the juices from it.

Her reasoning for sucking on the pickle like that was to tease and entice him to wanna be with her and only her.

After cruising for a little while Slim pulled in this vacant lot right next to this body shop where he use to get his cars spray painted at. The shop was closed because it was so late at night.

As they begin listening to Stevie wonder's Ribbon In They Sky they started to reminiscing about past times, and began talking about things they'd like to do in the future..... Slim begin to roll a joint.

"Uhhhh, you aint finna smoke that while I'm in here," she bodly said. "Don't worry I aint gone lace it," he said. "It don't matter if you lace it or not, you aint finna smoke that while I'm in here," she said. "Am a crack the window," he said. "You gone have my clothes smelling like weed," she said. "I told you am a crack the window," he said. "Fuck it gone head," she said.

He finish rolling up the joint and sat fire to it. He inhaled and exhaled the smoke harshly, which instantly boosted his dope high.

This shit a bomb he thought to himself.

He begin to try to convince her for sex, she still wasn't interested.

After he finished the joint he downed a half bottle of Champagne.

As he was downing the Champagne he visualized her and him fucking, and sucking each other.

He begin rubbing on her titties.....

"Stop boy don't put you hands on my titties I aint no ho. I don't get down like that," she said.

He then grabbed her left tittie. She snatched his hand away from her titties.

"Drop me off, drop me off," she said.....

In a frustrating sex craving rage he locked his car doors, ripped off her shirt as she begin yelling, kicking, and screaming.

He upped a .38 outta his jacket pocket, and told her "bitch shut the fuck up". And she immediately shut the fuck up.

Tears begin to roll down her face as he snatched off the rest of her clothes, then her panties in a storming rage.

He forced her to bend over the front seat and swiftly unbutton his pants and pulled them down to his knees craving for her pussy.

He tried to force feed her pussy his dick but it didn't work because her pussy was to tight, his dick was to big to get in.

She continued silently crying and pleading inside her heart and mind for him to stop, but he didn't.

With the gun in his left hand he spat in his right hand and rubbed it on the tip of his dick for lubrication.

He worked on getting his dick in her pussy. After a minute the tip of his dick finally slipped in. As he slowly worked his dick in and out her pussy to get it wet he began thinking to himself, damn this ho pussy tight as hell.

Once her inner juices begin flowing within he commence to slamming his dick in and out her pussy in a furious rage as she continued crying.

To him it seemed as if every stroke her pussy got weter and weter.

After the eighth pump he put the gun in his jacket pocket, and squeezed her waist, stopped pumping, and held his dick in her pussy until his entire nut was released in her guts.

He took his dick out, and grabbed her by the shoulders and turned her body around to face him.

"Please, please, please stop," she cried out to him.

He back hand slapped her with his left hand.....

"Shut up Bitch," he said.

She did exactly what he said. He pulled the gun back outta his jacket and put it to her head.

"Bitch suck this dick," he said. "Please, please, don't do this," she cried out. "Bitch suck this dick before I kill you," he said.

She begin crying even harder and pouting like a little kid, as her life flashed before her eyes she wrapped her lips around his dick.

She begin to suck his dick like never before. The wetness of her mouth, combined with her deep throat, and his high made it feel so good that he instantly unleashed a globb of nut down her throat as she swallowed it all.....

"Bitch get in the back seat," he said. "Please, please let me leave," she cried out.

He slapped her busting her bottom lip. She jumped in the back seat frightened of what he'd do if she didn't do what he told her to do.

She got on the back seat face down crying, laying flat on her stomach as he begin raping her in the ass.

She'd never felt so much pain in her life. He never felt so much pleasure in his life.

As he begin nutting it was as he visualized the skies filled with fire works similar to the fourth of July.....

He pushed her outta the car, and threw her clothes on top of her.

He smashed off listening to I'm Never Gone Leave Your Love, by Barry White.

At that very moment Slim felt as if he ruled the world. He loved the power he achieved from raping her.....

As Roxanne sat in the lot scared to death putting on her clothes a car drove pass slowly.

It was two individuals in the car, an old lady and her daughter coming from church.....

"Mom it's a lady in that lot naked," the little girl said. "Hush up now it aint nobody in no lot naked," the old lady said. "It is, it is, we need to go back and help her," the little girl said.

Her mother looked at her and seen the sincerity in her words, and pulled over.

"Girl if you have me to go back and it's not a naked woman there lord knows what am a do to you when we get home," the old lady said.....

She made a u-turn and went back to see if there really was a naked woman. As she pulled up to the lot Roxanne ran to her car with no shoes or shirt on nothing but her skirt with her hands over her titties crying, "please help me, please help me".

She jumped into the back seat of the four door car.....

"Oh my God, what happen to you," the old lady said historically. "He raped me," Roxanne cried out in a loud voice.

The old lady immediately drove off. Her and her daughter was in shock, they'd never experience being in a situation like that before.

Nervous, scared, unfocused, and not being able to drive right the old lady told Roxanne we gotta get you some clothes and take you to the hospital, and report this to the police.

"No, no police," Roxanne said with authority.

Roxanne didn't wanna get the police involved cuz she knew Slim was a ViceLord, and she knew what ViceLords would do to her if they found out she told the police on one of their members.....

"Please just take me home," Roxanne said frantically. "You sure you don't want me to take you to my home and get you cleaned up first," the old lady asked? "Naw please just take me home," Roxanne said. "Where do you live," the old lady asked?

Roxanne gave her, her address.

The rest of the ride all three of their minds was filled with sick satanic thoughts, as each individual remained silent.....

Once the old lady pulled up in front of Roxanne's house she looked at her feeling sorry and sad for her.....

"You sure you'll be okay," the old lady ask? "I'm going to be alright," Roxanne said with tears running down her face.....

Roxanne got out the car with her hands over her breast running to her door step. She rung the doorbell twice then her grandmother let her in as she feel to floor crying out, "he raped me".....

The old lady and her daughter rode home crying, and mentally thanking God that they'd never been attacked or raped before.....

Roxanne's grandmother and the rest of the family pleaded with her to tell the cops but she never did. Roxanne didn't want to jeopardize the safety of herself and her family.....

A couple days later Roxanne's family sent her to live in Atlanta with her aunt Rachel.....

A few days later Phill pulled up to Slim and Double J's joint, and parked in the middle of the street, and bailed outta the car.....

"Yous a stupid motherfucker, you done went and raped that girl. Do you know how much time rapes carry. Nigga aint no ViceLord gotta rap no ho's. Shiit we got ho's throwing us the pussy," Phill said, as he ran back to his car and smashed off burning rubber.....

Double J looked at slim with a frown on his face with curiousity running through his head.

"Man what the fuck is Phill talking about," Double J asked? "I don't know what that nigga tripping about," Slim said. "What the fuck he talking about somebody got raped," Double J said. "I told you I don't know what the fuck that nigga talking about," Slim said.

Later on that day Phill came through and politely closed Double J and Slim down. He took their joint and gave it to one of the universal elites. Phill was tired of Double J and Slim bullshit. They wasn't paying him his g a week. They was leaving their workers in jail wasn't bonding them out. Nor was they standing on nation business. Then, and then this nigga Slim went and raped a ho.....

Phill found out about the rape through Roxanne's lil cousins that was Renegade ViceLords. Roxanne's cousins was shorties, they wasn't experienced in gun slanging yet, so they hollered at Phill to see if Phill would violate Slim. Phill lied and told them he'd violate them if they made sure she didn't press charges..... Roxanne never press charges.....

Now Slim and Double J didn't have a joint to sell their dope on; Slim was mad at Double J for the money he fucked up in the past. Double J was mad at Slim for commiting that rape. Both of them was mad at Phill for taking their joint.

Slim and Double J didn't talk to each other for almost a week.

Slim ended up going over Double J's crib to get back some of his belongings.

Double J and Slim ended up making back up.

They went to this dope spot on the low end that suppose to had some good dope.....

For the first time in life Slim shot dope into his veins. The rush felt better than sex, snorting dope, smoking lace joints, or any other thing he'd experienced in life..... From that day forth Slim felt the true meaning of high til I die, because Slim knew he'd forever be a dopefiend.....

CHAPTER 5

Months later, January, 1972

S lim and Double J had become straight up dopefiends. Majority of their cars was confiscated by the repo man. All their jewelry, leathers, and almost everything else they owned were sold or either pawn.

They had been accustom to making fast money, and spending it fast; they had an expensive cost of living. But by them steady spending fast, and not making it fast no more the money the did possess started to become extinct......

They had resorted to doing whatever it took to get high; they was on some straight dope fiend shit.

Slim had begun doing a little pimping to get money to buy dope. Double J was against soliciting women. Although Double J was true dopefiend he still respected women.

One night Double J and Slim had finished doing some petty hustling. Double J decided to spend a night at Slim's crib,

Double J usually didn't spend nights out, he'd go home to his wife each night, but not this night.....

The next morning Double J woke up outta his sleep as the sun shined on his face.

Double J went into the bathroom to take a piss, and then went to Slim's room with one thing on his mind, getting some dope.

As he walked to Slim's bedroom he noticed that the bedroom door was partially opened. He didn't want to knock just in case they were asleep. So he looked in it to see if they were woke; and yes they were wide awoke.....

To Double J surprise there were Slim, Slim's white chick Angie, and two black women Reese and Tricey.....

There Slim stood with his shirt off, face and head looking like he aint shaved in years nodding, and shooting dope into his veins.

The three women was on the bed doing the nasty..... Angie was on all fours while Reese tortured her pussy from the back with this big black strap on dildo, as Tricey was on her knees holding Angie head to her pussy. It was as she was forcing her to eat her pussy.

"Bitch stop acting like you aint up with it and perform for the customers," Slim said.

Slim had turned innocent Angie out to a drug fiend, and a prostitute.

Double J bust in the room.

"Lord, what the fuck is you on. You done turned your main girl into a ho," Double J said. "Shes my bottom bitch," Slim said. "But that damn girl is four months pregnant, and you got her selling pussy to other women," Double J said.

The three ladies kept doing what they was doing, as if Slim or Double J wasn't even there.

"Nigga do you want to fuck her," Slim asked? "Naw man you know I'm married, but let me get some of that dope," Double J said.

Slim gave Double J the needle as he watched the girls sexing he shot dope into his veins.....

CHAPTER 6

S lim started robbing solo. Sometimes Slim would stick people up by himself cuz he didn't want to share the profit with Double J or nobody else.

Slim was from the west side, so he'd go to the south side and rob cuz didn't nobody really know him out south.

Late at night he'd catch women walking by themselves on streets were their wasn't very much traffic, and rob them for everything.

One time he robbed this young Mexican lady that didn't speak very much English on a dark street in back of a high school.

After robbing her she begin cursing him out in Spanish, he didn't speak any Spanish but he could tell that she was saying some foul shit cuz of her body language.

Within a rage of anger he forced her in his car at gun point and pulled her into the nearest alley.

He begin punching her in her face like it was a heavy weight professional boxers match until she was knocked unconscious.

He undressed her slowly with ease as this was his actual girlfriend, and as if he was getting ready for love making.

Once undressed while she was sprawled out over the front seats unconscious he paused for a second checking out her flawless body in which made his dick get hard as a brick. Violently, sexually crazed, within a frustrating erotic craving he took the pussy.

After nutting in the pussy he turned her over and took her booty.

Afterwards he dressed her and easily laid her in the alley behind a big garbage can.

6'oclock the next morning she awoke from the barking of dogs.

Slowly she stood up feeling the pain of her battered face, and the tissue in her pussy and ass that were torn.

As she slowly begin limping up the alley she seen this man pulling out his garage; he was a police officer on his way to work.

She flagged him down, and after seeing her bloody face he immediately put the car in park got out and helped her get into the passenger seat of his car.

Once she was in he showed her his badge. She felt a great sign of relief.

He then drove her to the County hospital to be examined by a doctor. On the way there she told him the horrifying story about what had happen to her last night. Well atleast the part she'd remember before actually going unconscious..... The officer was so pissed off that if he'd ever caught the individual who'd did that to her, he wouldn't have to worry about going to jail. He'd probably shoot and kill him on sight.....

The doctor's examination showed that she'd been beating, raped in her vagina, and anal.

The doctor gave her twelve stitches in three different parts of her face.

The officer then took her to the police station to file a report.

Once they made it within the police station all the other officers stared at her in silence.

The officer winded up filing a police report, and taking pictures of her bruises.

She told the truth within the report.....

The report stated that she'd been robbed, and abducted into a red Chevy Impala and took into an alley beating unconscious, and left within an alley. All these things was done by a mask gun man.....

Slim wasn't a dummy, the same night he burned up that red Chevy Impala. He didn't give a fuck about that car it was stolen steamer.....

After that night over the course of a month Slim had committed four more rapes. Three mask and one unmask. So know the authorities had a sketch of what he looked like. But a sketch wasn't the same as an actual picture. As a matter of fact the individual that did the sketching didn't do a good job on making it look like Slim.

Slim continued hanging out with Double J robbing, theiving, and pimping Angie, and doing whatever else it took to support his dope habit.....

Slim lived a double life that no one knew of. No one never knew that Slim had secretly turned into a raper man.....

Slim started to go up to the University of Chicago late night to prey on the women coming from night school. At first Slim couldn't rob or rape any of the women because the university's security cops would patrol the university frequently.

Before long Slim studied and learned the time the university security cops would patrol certain areas of the university.

One night after the students exited the first entrance of the school which was on a side street Slim seen her. A red head stood almost 6 feet, make up was flawless, walked like she was auditioning for a beauty pageant that she would definitely win.

Slim couldn't do nothing to her because there were to many other students around.

He ended up stalking her for a few days until one night he caught her walking up the street by herself.

He walked up to her unmasked. She seen him coming towards her, she thought he was getting ready to strike up a conversation in order to get a date or something. She was interested because Slim wasn't a bad looking guy although he was a dopefiend.

As Slim made it to her he upped a chrone .44.

"Bitch you bet not say a word or I'm a kill your ass," he said fierce and sincere. "Oh my gosh, oh my gosh, take whatever you want," she said as she handt him her purse. "Just please don't hurt me." "Bitch shut up and follow me, I aint gone hurt you," Slim said.

Slim walked her to his car under gun point and forced her in.

Once they got into the car and he drove off she pleaded for him not to hurt her.

"I told you I aint gone hurt you," he said.

In the back of her mind she knew he was lying. What else would an individual abduct someone at gun point for within the night time.

I hope the police pull on the side of us, or pull us over for a traffic violation, she thought to herself.

Once they were far away from the campus he pulled over and duct taped her mouth, handcuffed her hands together from the back, the same exact way the police do it, and blindfolded her.....

He drove her on the other side of town to his grandfathers home.

Once he made it to his grandfathers home pulled up in the garage, which was in the back of the house.

He escorted her from the garage, and took her to the basement. The neighbors couldn't see what was going on because of the wooden fences that surrounded the garage and the back of the house.

In her heart and mind she cried out for him to let her free.....

Once he got her in the basement he made her get on her knees as he uncuffed her hands then tied up her hands and feet with cords, leaving the blinfold on her eyes, and the duct tape around her mouth.

She'd never been so scared in her life.....

Slim then went upstairs to the second floor to check on his grandfather whom was sound asleep.

His grandfather was 88 years old. He had caught a disease when he was 80 that made him blind. His grandfather didn't have very much company; besides the nurses that would come to check on him each morning, bathe him, feed him, and other things of that nature. He'd even bribe a few nurses into having sex with him.

His grandfather lived in, and owned a two flat building.

Slim figured that his grandfather's basement would be a good place to keep the female he kidnapped. Slim knew that he was the only one whom had keys to the basement, and that his grandfather didn't have company besides nurses, and that his grandfather couldn't get up and move around on his own so therefore nobody would be coming into the basement.

Even if Slim's grandfather did have lots of company his grandmother wouldn't let nobody in the basement, cuz his grandfather use to be an gangster back in his younger days, and kept alot of guns in the basement he had from back in the days.

For years his grandfather stop renting out the first floor to tenants, because some tenants didn't pay their rent on time.....

After Slim seen his grandfather was sound asleep he went back into the basement and stared at this pretty young hot white lady he kidnapped.

He couldn't stop staring at her. Although she was tied up blindfolded and her mouth was duct tape he still enjoyed watching her beautiful features.

Slim begin to slowly undress his victim. She begin crying as tears ran down her face thinking to herself like damn, he finna rape me.

She tried to move her body struggling for him not to rape her but it was like a mission impossible. As he slowly undressed her his dick got hard on the sight of her freshly shaved pussy.

As he upped his dick and entered her pussy with force it was like heaven on earth for him. To her it was like a living hell.

As he begun taking the pussy from her he started slapping on her ass cheeks calling her every disrespectful name in the book. In a sick sexual perverted way he was really enjoying himself.

All night he did almost every sexual act known to men from fingering her pussy, and ass, sucking her titties. Sticking his dick in her pussy and ass. And for the first time in life he stuck his tongue up a woman's ass.....

~~~~~~~~~

A couple of days later, on a cold winter's night, Slim and Double J was sitting in a car in Garfield Park finishing shooting and snorting dope, and smoking lace joints, wondering to themselves what they could do to make some more money to get high.....

"Lord, what we gone do to get some more dope," Slim asked Double J? "I don't know, that's a good question," Double J said.

Both men remained silent for a brief moment enjoying their highs and trying to figure out how they was gonna get some more dope.

"Lets steal some cars," Double J said. "Hell naw man that's a headache. First we gotta find some cars to steal, then we gotta find somebody to buy the parts off it," Slim said. "Well when you come up with something better then let me know," Double J said.

"I'm tired of stealing cars, boosting clothes, and pimping. All that shit takes to long, I be needing instant money, I love to get high," Slim said. "Yeah I feel you, cuz I'm tired of the same shit. I like robbing dope spots, cuz you get money and dope right then and there. But we done robbed damn near every spot out west. And the ones we didn't rob was because they had guns on it or they was patting us down," Double J said.

"Let's order a pizza," Slim said.....

Double J turned his head directly facing Slim looking at him like he was crazy.....

"Damn you went from trying to figure out how to get some money to ordering a pizza," Double J said sarcastically. "I'm talking about robbing the pizza man," Slim said. "Robbing the pizza man is burn up, everybody been doing it. Majority of the pizza men don't even have that much money on them, just in case they do get robbed," Double J said. "They gone have some money on them, whatever he have it'll be enough to get some dope and we gone get something to eat all for free," Slim said.

Double J begin laughing and thinking to himself this nigga Slim is silly.

"The average pizza man aint gone come to certain hoods," Double J said. "Yeah I know we gone go to one of them nice ass hoods and call him, and give him one of the addresses. Once he make it to the address, before he even get a chance to knock on the door here come me to take his shit," Slim said.

"Sounds like a good plan to me, so uhhh what we waiting on," Double J said.....

Slim pulled off and rode for about twenty minutes to a hood that wasn't ghetto.

He pulled on a super quiet block and got the address from the house that was on the corner. They then went to the pay phone and ordered two large cheese pizza's with most of the toppings.

As they went back they parked in front of the house they gave the address to it was as both of them could actually taste and smell the pizza.

They couldn't wait to get paid and wrap their lips around them pizza's.

In no time flat the pizza man was pulling up, and parking right behind them.

They seen a hispanic looking dude get out the car with two big pizza's in his hands.

Slim jumped out the driver's side of the car with gun in hand.

"Bitch give me them motherfucking pizza's, and empty your pocket's," Slim said.....

The pizza man did exactly what Slim said, with no hesitation, scared to death.

"Bitch get in the car and drive off," Slim said after robbing him.

The pizza man got in his car and pulled off, damn near causing a car collision once he made it to the intersection.

Slim got into the car, pulled off going in the opposite direction from the pizza man.

Once they made it back to the hood they parked and begin eating pizza and counting the money.....

"Damn Lord this pizza is a bomb," Double J said. "It came from Home Run Inn," Slim said.

Slim continued counting the money.

"We got two hundred and eighty dollars," Slim said. "Give me my half," Double J said.

Slim counted out a hundred and forty and passed it to Double J.

What Double J didn't know was that Slim only pulled out some of the money outta his pocket. He played for the rest.

They continued eating pizza on their way to the dope spot.....

They spent majority of that two-eighty getting high that night.....

~~~~~~~~~

Two days later while Slim was asleep he had a dream that two midget women, one was black, one was white was taking turns sucking on his dick.

When he was about to unleash a load of nut he awoke to the reality of his girl Angie laying there ass hole naked sucking on his dick; and it felt so good to him.

As he unleashed his nut down Angies throat he begin rubbing on her titties and pregnant belly.

Afterwards they both stood up as he looked her straight in the eyes and told her "see that's why I love you so." Then he kissed her on her left cheek and hugged her tightly.

They ended up getting high, then getting dressed and going to a breakfast joint.

While they sat at the table eating breakfast a glimpse of the woman's face he had tied up in his grandfather's basement flashed in his mind.

Damn I done left that lady tied up in the basement for two days with nothing to eat, Slim thought to himself.

Slim and Angie ate and then Slim immediately dropped her off at home.

On his way to his grandfather's home he stopped at McDonalds to buy the lady he'd kidnapped something to eat.

Once he made it to his grandfather's basement his victim could hear his footsteps and begin yelling and crying, but no one could hear her cries because of the duct tape around her mouth. She surely thought that eventually he'd kill her.

For the last two days she'd been living a non-fiction horror story.

She'd tried to get loose to escape but always came up unsuccessful.

Slim took the blindfold off, and said "how are you doing sleeping beauty."

Her eyes got wide as she became scarder than ever by this maniac.

"I'm going to take this tape off your mouth to feed you. If you start to make any noise I'm putting the tape back on your mouth and you wont eat," he said.

She nodded her head up and down in agreement.

He put the blindfold back on.

As soon as he took the tape off her mouth she begin yelling to the top of her lungs, "somebody please help me, somebody please."

Before she could finish yelling he put the tape back around her mouth.

"I guess you don't wanna eat," he said sinisterly.

He pulled off his pants got on his knees and begun rubbing her clitoris with his left hand and fondling his own dick with his right hand.

As Slim begin to get erect and the moisture of her pussy started to be felt on his hand, he got behind her and shoved his dick in her pussy.

The tightness combined with the moisture and him being high felt great.

He slammed his dick in and out her pussy showing no remorse for it.

Afterwards he went up to the second floor and checked on his grandfather. His grandfather was doing okay.

He went back to the basement.

He begin whispering in his victims ear; "I'm going to ask you one more time do you want to eat something."

She begin shaking her head up and down.

"I'f I take this tape off your mouth and your start hollering and shit am a make sure you don't eat for a long ass time," he said.

He took the tape off her mouth, she didn't say a word, she was starving, and she knew that no matter how loud she'd holler no one would probably hear her.

As she opened her mouth wide all Slim could do was visualize his dick going in and out her mouth.

Within a split second decision he decided to use some type of tool to feed her cuz if he would've use his hands she might try to bite off some of his fingers.

He looked over at the bar-b-que grill, walked over and opened it up.

There sat a tool used to grip and flip meat.

He went to the sink rinsed the tool and went back over and begin feeding her the cold McDonalds.

She ate the food like she was a starven little kid from one of them third world countries.

After she finished eating she begin to cry out to him; "Please, please let me go I'll give you anything, my family is rich, they'll make sure you get compensated for letting me free."

He put the tape back over her mouth thinking about the compensation money.

I'f I let this ho go and try to get compensated my ass gone be in jail forever, he thought to himself.

He forced her to the floor laying flat on her stomach and dived in the pussy full force. Slamming his dopefiend dick in and out of her tight pussy as hard as he possibly could while admiring the view of the way her ass cheeks would jiggle each time he'd bounce up and down on her.....

~~~~~~~~~~

Slim and Double J's dope habits had started as a monkey on their back and turned into a real live Silver Back Gorilla.

They begin robbing any and everybody from cab drivers, pizza men, corner stores, hood restaurants, dope dealers, old people and all.

Every single day they'd rob many different people, just to get high.....

A month after the robbing spree begin Chicago police were on the hunt for Double J and Slim cuz they'd robbed so many people. Some of the corners stores, hood restaurants, they'd robbed more than once, and witnesses had positively indentified Double J and Slim.

Now Double J and Slim were on the run.

Double J's wife had filed for a divorce. She didn't wanna be with no dopefiend ass nigga. So Double J was living from house to house. Majority of the people he lived with was some of his dopefiend buddies.

Slim on the other hand had told Angie to move in with one of her friends. And he himself stayed in his grandfather's building.

Slim assumed that no one from the hood knew where his grandfather lived, so he figured his grandfather's home would be a good place to hide out at.

A couple weeks went by Slim had just finished shooting up some dope and went back to his grandfather's basement.

He fed his victim; after she finished eating he put the tape back over her mouth. He got naked took off her blindfold to finally let her see his full body naked.

He laid her flat on her stomach and went off in her ass for the first time. She yelled, screamed, and cried crocodile tears.

Slim couldn't hear her yells, screams, or cries because of the tape around her mouth.....

In the midst of Slim having his way with her ass. The basement door flew open..... "freeze police."

Almost thirty police officers flooded the room.

The police immediately snatched Slim off his victim handcuffed him, and told him that he was being charged with twenty seperate counts of arm robbery.

They untied the kidnapped woman; to the police she seemed to be almost lifeless with her booty bleeding as if she were stabbed in it.

Once they took the duct tape of her mouth she jumped up crying, "Oh my gosh thank you for rescuing me," she said.

They wrapped a blanket around her as she told her non-fiction horror story.

As the police searched the basement they found all seven of the old guns his grandfather had and put them on Slim.

Now Slim had twenty counts of robbery. A kidnapping, a sexual assualt, and seven unlawful use of weapons. He was never getting outta jail. And when and if he did he'd be an old man.

Come to find out the lady he'd kidnapped, and raped repeatidly was Suzan Armstrong, a twenty seven year old English teacher.

On the ride to the police station the police beat his ass. Gave him two black eyes, a busted nose, and knocked out two of his teeth.

Once he made it to the police station they ended up putting him in a line up.

Five more business owners picked him outta a line up for robbing there businesses.

One other woman picked him out of a line up for raping her; she was the one he raped with no mask on.

Once he made it to the Cook County jail he felt the full effect of being dope sick.

He sat in the bull pen crying out to Allah, father of the universe as he threw up his guts it was as twenty maniacs were all poking away at his stomach with small sharp objects. He'd never felt so much pain in his life.

Once he finally made it to the dec the guys screened him to see if he was gang affiliated.

Once they found out he was a ViceLord they checked to see if he had any status.

Once they found out he wasn't a universal elite they showed him the ropes introduced him to all the brother's.

They next day they gave him a knife and put him on the ViceLords security.

A few days later Slim got in touch with his grandfather and Angie. His grandfather start sending money, and Angie begin visiting on his visiting days.

After a few weeks of being in the county Slim begin to notice the ViceLords and everybody else on the dec start straying away from him.....

One morning Slim didn't awake for breakfast he over slept. While asleep three big dudes came into his dark cell and begin beating the shit out of him with men made weapons..... Slim didn't stand a chance on fighting back.

One man took his pants off and took his booty.

Slim screams was like an horryfying echo, as the tissue in his booty hole got torn.

~~~~~~~~~

The ViceLords and all other gangs under the fin was against homosexuality; therefore a ViceLord or any other gang under the fin wouldn't rape another man, or women. But it's other gangs that didn't give a fuck about homosexuality; especially if a man let another man rape him. The other gangs that wasn't fin ball looked at it as if a nigga let another nigga rape him then he needed to be raped. Majority if not all gangs in Chicago was against raping women. That's why they raped him so he could see how it felt to be raped.

Afterwards Slim ran to the ViceLords, body filled with pain, barely able to see because of his eyes being covered with blood, crying out for the ViceLords assistance.

The ViceLord and everybody on the dec laughed at him, as if he was a comedian on stage, and they were the audience.

Slim looked around crying out for help, as they laughed, he couldn't believe what was going on. The dramatization was that of a horror flick for Slim.

One ViceLord shouted out, "we don't fuck with no raper man."

Slim then ran to the c/o's. The c/o's called 10 10 and within seconds a gang of c/o's flew on the dec whupping the inmates ass and putting the dec on lock down, and escorted Slim to the jails hospital.

Slim received seventeen stitches and ten staples. The staples were in his head. The stitches was in various places in his body including his ass, he got fucked up real bad.

Slim told the c/o's he didn't know what happen. He didn't know who did that to him. Slim didn't believe in telling the police shit.

Slim was escorted back to the dec which was still on lock down to get his things.

Slim went to a few of the ViceLords cells that was universal elites.

"Lord, ya'll gone let them niggas get down on me like that," Slim said. "You know we don't get down like that," one of the universal elites said, through the cell door. "Like what," Slim asked? "We heard you was locked up for raping ho's. We against that Lord. We aint ever honoring you as no ViceLord no more..... Shiiit since you been raped you're a faggot now. Where ever you go in jail you aint gone get no respect for letting them niggas rape you."

Slim went to other ViceLords cells and they didn't even wanna talk to him, disgusted by him being a raper man, and letting them niggas rape him.

Once Slim made it to P.C right than and there he seen two of his homies from the streets; they had fucked up some people drugs, and commisary and checked into P.C., cuz they couldn't pay them.

Slim immediately noticed it was alot of faggots in P.C. he didn't like being around the faggots.....

After a couple of months in jail Slim's grandfather died. That was so fucked up for him. His grandfather was the only family he ever really had. He never knew his real dad. His mom had been dead for many years, she was killed in a car accident when he was a kid. The rest of his family lived down south, and the little family he had that lived in Chicago was phony ass hell.

He couldn't even attend his grandfather's funeral cuz it costed $1,500 for the county jail to escort inmates to funerals.....

A couple months after Slim's grandfather's death Double J was found in an abandon building dead, with a needle stuck in his arm; he died of an overdose of dope.....

Slim came to find out that his girl Angie was fucking around with a nigga from the hood.

It was as Slim, and his entire world was beginning to fall apart.....

CHAPTER 7

A ngie begin feeling labor pains.....
"My water just broke, I'm going into labor," Angie told her lover Todd.

Todd eyes got wide.

Todd immediately drove her to the hospital.

After seven hours of labor Angie gave birth to a new born baby.

Once the baby was released from Angie the female doctor stated "it's a beautiful little girl, she's beautiful enough to be a queen."

The baby weighed 6 pounds, and 2 ounces.

Angie had stop getting high when she was seven months pregnant so the baby wouldn't have any drugs in her system so DCFS wouldn't take the baby from her; therefore the baby came out healthy.

Angie looked in her beautiful little baby's eyes and it was as she could see the queen her daughter was destine to be, so she named her Queeny.

Queeny had gray eyes; usually when a baby is born with gray eyes they don't remain that color they change to hazel green, brown, even blue as the baby gets older. Queeny had brown hair, high yellow skin. You could look at her and tell she was mixed with white and black.

A couple weeks after the baby was born Angie took Queeny to the County jail to see her dad.

Slim came out in the visiting room and seen this baby in her hands, he didn't even know that she had gave birth.....

"Here is your daughter," Angie said, through the tiny air holes in the glass.

Slim instantly begin smiling looking through the glass of the visiting cage as Angie took the blanket off the baby's face.

"She so cute, what is her name," Slim asked? "I named her Queeny because she's destine to be a queen," Angie said.

"I didn't even know you had the baby. When did you have her," Slim asked? "A couple weeks ago," Angie said.

"Shes so cute she looks just like you," he said. "She look more like you to me," Angie said.

As the baby opened her eyes it was as he could see the sunrise.

Reality started to set in, Slim begin thinking to himself, like damn I'm never getting outta jail, my child is going to be a bastard.....

The visit didn't last long cuz Slim couldn't stand to be around Angie and Queeny knowing he'd never see the streets again in order to actually be a part of their lives.....

~~~~~~~~

Angie and her boyfriend Todd begin living in this studio apartment on the north side of Chicago.

Angie had stop getting high when she was seven months pregnant, but once she had Queeny she started right back getting high at an all time high..... She always had regrets on letting Slim turn her out to be an addict, cuz she knew drugs was her downfall, but she loved to get high.

Todd and Angie had devoted their lives to the usage of drugs.

One late night Todd was coming back home from the twenty four hour liquor store.

As Todd opened the door someone pushed him into their apartment.

Todd turned around on the verge of laying hands on whomever pushed him. But turned around and seen that big ass gun.

"Nigga step back," the gunman said fiercly in a Jamican accent.

Once Todd stepped all the way in the apartment Angie seen the gunman step in behind Todd as she yelled out, "we finna die."

The gun man immediately shut the door leaving it unlock. He then put his index finger over his mouth sushing Angie.....

"Be cool, and be quiet I aint gone hurt ya'll. I'm just gone rob ya'll and leave ya'll here tied up, so ya'll can't call the police once I leave," the gunman said sincerly.

Rob us, we aint got shit, Todd thought to himself.

The robber took off his hoody, he was black as hell with Jamican dreeds in his head.

Aw shit this is one of these crazy ass Jamicans, Todd thought to himself.

Todd instantly begin sizing him up just in case he slip up, he'd try to knock the gun outta his hand and take it from him.

The gunman stood about 5.7, and Todd could tell that he had been to the joint before cuz he was swole to death.

Within seconds another man dressed in black came in. He looked as if he could be the other guys big brother.

The second man came right in and blindfolded Todd and Angie. He then made them get on their knees, duct tape their hands behind their back, duct tape their legs together, and put duct tape around their mouths.....

Angie and Todd wasn't worried about what the robbers would do to them, because they honestly believed that the robbers would only rob them and then leave. Todd and Angie was more worried about how they was going to get free from that duct tape.

The first robber begin to notice Queeny sitting in her rocking chair asleep; as he stepped closer to her she awoke opening her beautiful eyes. She's so cute, the robber thought to himself.

Both man upped knives and begin stabbing away at Todd and Angie's flesh as Queeny watched emotionless because she was only a baby and didn't know or understand what was going on.

Outside it begin to rain and thunder as the so called robbers continued stabbing Todd and Angie up over thirty times a piece, leaving, them for dead.

Within minutes the killers left the two bodies there laid out in there own puddles of blood that filled the carpet.

They left Queeny laying there in her rocking chair smiling listening to a Fisher Price toy that played baby music.

As they left they didn't bother to take anything because they wasn't robbers, the were sent to kill. They ran out leaving the door open.

A few years earlier Todd use to buy dope from some Jamicans up north, but wind up having them front him some dope and he fuck the money up. He thought he'd never see the Jamicans again. But he was wrong, one of the Jamicans seen him coming out of their apartment building, and sent killers to kill.

The next morning one of the neighbors had been in and out her apartment all that morning for various reasons and noticed that their door had been open all that morning.

The first time she seen the door open it really wasn't any concern to her. But after seeing it open for hours she knocked on it to see if everything was alright.

After not getting a response from her hard knock she opened it and seen the bleeding dead bodies and begin screaming. It was as the screams echoed from blocks and blocks.

She ran to her apartment scared to death as if a killer was actually after her.

She went into her apartment locked the door, and put the chain on it. Ran to the phone and dialed 911.

After the fourth ring the dispatcher answered.....

"Hello, this Chicago police dispatcher may I help you."

"It's two dead people, I'ts two dead people," she said breathing heavy, crying, scared nervous. "Calm down mam, now can you repeat yourself," the dispatcher said. "Two of my neighbors are lying in there front room dead, somebody killed them," the lady said. "Mam give me the address and I'll send help over immediately," the dispatcher said. "1170 N. Jarvis," the lady said. "What apartment or floor," the dispatcher asked? "Apartment 2B", she said. "Help will be over shortly," the dispatcher said.

"Did you see who did these murders," the dispatcher asked? "No damnit I don't want to talk, send the police over here," the lady said.

Before the dispatcher could say another word she'd hung up the phone.

This was a prominent white neighborhood therefore the police was there in no time.....

Two rookie cops entered the apartment first and became sick to there stomachs. As all the other police entered and seen the dead bodies it was nothing to them they'd seen dead bodies many times before.

One of the rookie cops which was a white woman in her mid-twenties begin crying "why, why, why would somebody do this," as tears ran down her face.....

They took Queeny to the hospital to see if everything was alright with her Queeny was okay.....

The authorities tried to find Queeny's family, and came up unsuccesful.

Angie's family mainly lived in other states, and didn't even know a child existed. Those that lived in Chicago, or nearby Chicago didn't want to have anything to do with the baby because she was partially black, they was racist as hell. They even disowned Angie when she first begin fucking around with Slim. They felt like Angie had disgrace their family name.....

Once Slim found out about Angie being killed he felt like he had nothing else worth living for.....

The next morning after Slim found out about Angie a female officer came through doing the 11:00 A.M. count she immediately noticed that some of the two men cells only had one inmate in there which was fucking up her count, cuz she was use to counting by twos.

Slim was in the cell by himself he had no celly. His last celly had went home a couple days ago.

The woman c/o came to count Slim looked in his cell door and there Slim was asshole naked, hanging from a homemade rope he made from bed sheets.

The c/o begin instantly screaming. She started screaming so loud that she woke up everybody on the dec.

All the inmates begin looking outta the chuckhole of their cells doors, as the other c/o's rushed in to see what was going on.

Once the c/o's made it to her she said in a loud screeching voice, "he hung himself."

The c/o's instantly keyed the door open and took him down from the rope.

One c/o knew how to check his pulse. The c/o checked his pulse looked at the other officers with water in his eyes and said, "he's dead."

The other c/o got on his walky talky and called for doctor's to come and attend to Slim's body.

One of the other c/o's grabbed the big piece of paper that was taped to his stomach and read it out loud: That's one thing about life is that at the end of it we must all die, and I chose my own time to die, I'll see you in hell where my sinful soul will dwell.

The room got silent as his handwritten words was a reality check for the c/o's. They knew that one day we must all die.

Police ended up turning Queeny over to the custody of DCFS.

Within weeks this elderly lady that was a landlord in one of the building that Angie and Slim lived in together before had attended both Angie's and Slim's funeral and found out Queeny was in DCFS. The elderly lady tried to locate Slim's and Angie's family and she came to find out that neither Slim nor Angie's family didn't give a fuck about Queeny.....

The elderly lady, Christine took it upon herself to obtain custody of Queeny.

At first DCFS didn't wanna give Christine custody of Queeny cuz she was old, and because she wasn't married.

One of Christine's grandkids was lovers with the 27th ward alderman, and he helped Christine to obtain custody of Queeny.

Queeny brought joy and sunshine to Christines life. Christine had never been happier than she'd been in her entire sixty five years of living.....

Christine died at the age of seventy when Queeny was only five. When Christine died it was as a piece of Queeny died inside; although she was real young she still felt the pain of loosing Christine.

Queeny never knew her mom and dad or any of there family all she knew was Christine. Christine treated her as if she was her very own daughter.

After Christine's death none of her family members wanted to adopt Queeny.

One of Christine's daughter Roseline ending up taking custody of Queeny.

Roseline was Christine's only daughter that turned out bad.

Roseline was an alcholic, and tutted raw cocaine.

Inside of Roseline home smelled like a dead body was in there, Roseline didn't know or understand what clean meant. Roseline's house wasn't even fit for wild animals to live.....

Daily Roseline would beat Queeny for petty reasons.

Queeny cries from Roseline's beating would literally haunt her in her sleep. Some nights she couldn't sleep constantly awaking from nightmares of Roseline's beatings. Queeny always promised herself that if she ever had kids she'd show nothing but love, and would never put her hands on them under no circumstances.....

CHAPTER 8

A few years later..... Although Queeny was still experience difficulties with Roseline she had no other choice, because this is all the family she really had.....

Queeny maintained good grades in school, she was a real smart kid.

The only problem she had was that she got into many fights in school because they assumed she was white. The school she went to was populated by all blacks. Although she was mixed with white and black she mainly looked white. The immature kids would make racial slurs and continue picking on her.

She got tired of going through bullshit at home with Roseline, and at school with the kids bullying her, as she began starting fights beccoming the bully herself.

I'f anyone at school would create any problems she'd instantly start a fist fight with anybody releasing all her anger and frustration off on them. In no time she begin to get respect from the kids at school.....

King Phill would see Queeny walking to school some mornings. Phill would look at Queeny and feel sorry for her; Phill knew her story. He knew her mom, and dad was dead, and that Roseline was a drug addict.

Queeny knew Phill as well. Ever since she could remember within her young life Phill always help her out with Christmas gift's, school supplies amongst other things.....

One day while Queeny was walking to school alone he decided to walk her to school.

"Queeny slow down am a walk you to school," Phill said. "Why don't you drop me off in your car," Queeny said. "Somebody in my car I'm just gone walk you to school," he said.

Phill begin to pour his heart out to her, and give her a little game.

"I like seeing you go to school, go to college and do something with your life. You're destine for fortune and fame. Never settle for anything less than the best. Don't never let a man rule or ruin your life. Live your life like the queen of all queens," Phill said.....

~~~~~~~~~

When Queeny was twelve Roseline had became a prostitute.

One night Roseline went out on the ho stroll to sell some pussy and never came back.

People in the neighborhood assumed she was killed by a trick, but her dead body was never found, or no one didn't witness to her being killed, only assumptions.....

King Phill had his sister Rachel to get custody of Queeny.

Rachel was an alcoholic, but she didn't use drugs. And she took care of her business, doing the best she could to raise her own kids. Rachel had five kids of her own. Rachel two teenage boys were eighteen and seventeen years old, and her other three kids whom were girls ages were fifteen, thirteen, and eleven.

Queeny begin smoking weed with Tom and Paul; Rachels two sons, and hanging in the streets, a little, seeing the actions, and transactions of the ViceLords. She begin being infatuated with the ViceLord nation. The ViceLords showed out as far as selling dope and getting money. Most women are attracted to money. She was intigued by the mass amount of men that was representing V.L. They wore their hats to the left and dressed in the slickest gear.

There were many other gangs in Chicago, but the ViceLords was mostly adored by the women.....

Queeny didn't need any finance because Phill, and Rochelle made sure she was straight financially. But by her being young and dumb she begin to get involved in criminal activities not only for the extra money, but for the excitement as well.....

At the age fourteen Queeny and some of the niggas she went to high school with would go to clothing stores and steal. They'd do the theiving, while Queeny would be talking to the store workers for long periods of time as a distraction method. They'd take the clothing and sell them to dope dealers. The money was cool, but Queeny was full of greed and wanted more. She'd became victim to the fast life as fast living, and fast money.

Before long she begin selling dope with Tom and Paul. Tom, Paul, and Queeny knew that if Phill found out they'd be in deep shit. King Phill didn't want any of his family members using or selling drugs; but he didn't attempt to stop the men in his family from using or selling drugs, although he didn't like it. As far as the women were concerned he'd go crazy if he'd found out they were selling or using dope.

One day Phill notice that Queeny was hanging on one of the spots in the hood during school hours.

Phill begin snapping on Queeny. He told her that everytime school hours were in process she'd better be in school. And when she got outta school she still couldn't hang out on no dope spots.....

The same week he caught her hanging on one of the hoods dope spot, this time after school hours.

She made up an excuse claiming that she was passing by and begin talking to a nigga she go to school with. Phill told her that if she don't get her act together he'd stop giving her money. That was his way and other street niggas way of punishing people by ceasing to provide them with finance, but that didn't work. She continued to hang on the dope spots, and continued selling dope.....

At this time within Chicago majority of the dope spots were behind close doors; but Tom, and Paul dope house continued to get raided by the police, therefore they decided to start selling their dope on the corners. There for they wanted Queeny to work because the police wouldn't suspect her as the one selling the dope. The only problem is that she was a candidate for a stick up. She got robbed twice in one week.

Tom, and Paul came to the realization that she was still a little girl, and it wasn't no need for her to be out there. Tom, and Paul knew that she could get shot by the stick up man, catch a juvenille case, and alotta other bad shit could happen.

Tom, and Paul started telling her that she didn't have to sell dope, because they'd give her money and Phill would to, only if she behaved herself.

She'd told them that she enjoyed selling dope, which was the truth. She was selling dope partially for the money and partially for the thrill and art of it. The boys told her that the streets was cold and unfair. She then told them that if they didn't want her to work for them they'll be others that would let her work.

The boys knew in the back of there minds she was right. They both became upset that they even introduced her to this aspect of the street life.

So she wouldn't be on the spot they then started letting her go to the table to bag up dope; sometimes they'd be at the table with her, sometimes she'd do it by herself. The pay was greater for her and it was a less risk of her getting robbed or catching a case. And Phill would never find out about her going to the table.

One day Queeny was walking home from school through a dope spot which wasn't in doors it was out on the corner, and seen a member of the ViceLords shooting at a rival gang. This was her first time seeing a gun being shot, she liked the excitement.....

The night before at a party the ViceLords and G.D's got into a fight over one guy felt on a females ass. The two men ended up fighting. One man was a ViceLord, and the other one was a G.D. It led to a mass amount of both gangs fighting in the club.

The club had metal detectors therefore they couldn't get in with their guns or any other weapons. Once the crowd disbursed outta the club and went to their cars. One of the ViceLords opened fire and wounded one of the G.D.'s. He didn't die but he was seriously injured. Which led into a street war against the ViceLord and G.D's.

During this war she'd heard so much gun fire it became like music to her ears.

During this particular war she started carrying guns; not for her personal use but to only transport them for Tom, and Paul, or other members of the ViceLords. By her being a female it was less chance for the police to harass her than they would a man.

She liked carrying guns, she craved for the day she'd be able to squeeze the trigger of one.....

One time one of the guys that worked for her brothers, purchased a fully loaded .32 revolver from a dopefiend for forty dollars. Normally when an individual from the streets buys a gun they immediately shot it to see if it'll shoot with no defects, but he didn't, he wanted to wait until nightfall.

Queeny was there when he bought the gun. She wanted to hear how it would sound, she adored the sound of gunfire. He told her to wait to tonight and he'd let her shoot it.

Her eyes opened with amazement, thinking to herself I can't wait until tonight.

Later on that night he let her shot it, she thought it would be difficult to shoot, all along it was like chewing bubble gum.

The first shot felt and sounded so good to her that she unloaded all six shots into the sky.....

CHAPTER 9

A fter months progressed along the ViceLords and the G.D.s war had long cease. Now the ViceLords was into it with each other. The Insanes was into it with the Renegade ViceLords; this was unusual because all branches of ViceLord worked together. But one of the Insanes robbed one of the Renegades for 10,000 in drugs.....

Queeny wanted to be involved and do some shootings but they wouldn't let her because she was a female, and so young. In reality they didn't take her serious as far as doing any shootings.....

More and more Queeny would gaze at the skies viciously lusting for the day she could unload a gun. Not in the skies like she'd once did before but in a human being this time.

Although Queeny was so young, yet and still in her own heart and mind she felt as a queen over all.

Queeny knew the meaning of power and she wanted it in abundance.....

Once Queeny initially started bagging up dope for Tom, and Paul, she had stopped hustling directly on the dope spot, for a little while.....

One day Queeny started back hustling on Tom, and Paul's joint just to get a little extra money, and was robbed for the third time.

Once her brother's Tom, and Paul found out about it they told her once again to stay away from the dope spots, she didn't listen.....

Tom, and Paul got tired of their dope spots getting robbed so they start paying a man two hundred each day to stand on security with a gun just in case the stick up man came through; the security man shift would consist of twelve hours.

By this time Tom, and Paul had all sorts of poeple in play to run their dope spot. Tom and Paul basicly didn't do shit, but collect money.

One day Queeny decided to get up with Tom, and Paul's workers to take the security position of holding the gun just in case the stick up man came through.

She took this position for two reasons: To be in possession of the gun so she could bust it if the stick up man ever came through she could shoot the shit outta him or them. Also so she could show the guys that she had more heart than them.....

While standing on security she prayed that the stick up man would come through.

She took this security position on a saturday. She knew that if Phill caught her on the spot on a saturday she'd think of some lame excuse of why she was hanging on the spot, and knew she'd have less problems from Phill being that it wasn't a school day.

The security hours revolved around her curfew. The security hours were twelve hours a day. Usually 8:00 A.M.- 8:00 P.M., then 8:00 P.M.- 8:00 A.M. Her curfew was at 10:00 P.M. so she'd work the shift from 8:00 A.M.- 8:00 P.M.

She ended up working security on saturday and sunday.....

Sunday morning a stick up a man robbed the workers. By her being on security she suppose to make sure the stick up man didn't even get a chance to rob the workers, but he did.

As the stick up man ran to his car after robbing the workers she seen him running with his gun in hand as the workers yelled, "he just robbed me."

She unloaded a .38 into the back window of his car; she didn't hit him although she was really trying.

When this incident occured it was broad daylight, everyone seen it.

She immediately went to a house in the hood to stash the weapon and went home.

Although she didn't hit the stick up man she didn't find this out to later on.....

She sat at home dramitized, thinking that she'd shot and killed him, and that she'd be going to jail for a long ass time.....

The entire day it was the talk of the hood gossip, how Queeny young ass popped that pistol.

At this day and age in the 1990's you didn't have too many females shooting guns like the females in the 1980's. The women in the 1990's were more caught up in being pretty girls. Mainly dressing fresh, partying, and having fun.

Once Tom, and Paul heard about it they went home snapping on her.....

"Girl we give you money, and momma, and Phill give you money, and we let you go to the table for us. What the fuck was you even doing out there on security for a funky two hundred dollars," Tom said. "I wasn't doing it for the money. I was out there just in case the stick up man came through," Queeny said. "Why the fuck is you worried about the stick up man for," Paul asked? "Because Imma queen and I got my own ways of doing things," Queeny said. "Girl you done lost your motherfucking mind. A queen my ass, you betta hope that guy aint get shot or killed. I'f he did your ass gone be the queen of jail," Paul said.

The next morning King Phill had heard what she'd done. Phill knew it was Tom, and Paul's dope spot; therefore King Phill was intelligent enough to know that the Tom, and Paul had something to do with it, one way or the other.

Phill confronted Tom, and Paul and didn't even give them a chance to explain; Phill had both Tom, and Paul violated by other members of the ViceLord nation.

Phill wanted to beat Queeny's ass but he didn't because she was a girl. He was against putting his hands on females, especially a little girl in which he considered to be a part of his family.....

The next day Phill told Queeny to pack her shit she was moving. He took her to one of his other sisters house whom lived on the south side of town.....

After several weeks Queeny ran away from his sister's sheila crib.

Sheila was rude and disrespectful at the mouth, and to controlling. She knew if she didn't leave from Phill's sister Sheila's crib they would end up fighting.

Queeny went back to the westside to live with one of the girls she went to school went, Susan.

Queeny didn't have to many girl friends; because she was the true essence of a Tomboy, and mainly hung around with the guys. But her and Susan was real cool she knew her since grammer school. In grammer school she spent alot of time with Susan and her family. Once she got to high school she didn't hang out with her alot, she'd mostly kicked it with her in school.

She knew she couldn't stay with Susan's family for to long it'll only be temporarily, maybe for a few weeks, or a couple months at the most.

It was cool for Queeny to live with Susan, because Susan lived close to the school, and they had some of the same classes together.....

Once King Phill found out that Queeny was missing, the first thing came to his mind was that something bad had happen to her. Not once did it cross his mind that she'd ran away from home.

King Phill begin looking for Queeny relentlessly. He also told everyone he knew that if someone had any information of her whereabouts he'd pay heavily for that information.

A couple of days later one of Phill's tightest homies seen her going to school, and went and told Phill. Phill sat in his car outside of Queeny's high school awaiting on her to depart.

Once school was over he seen Queeny exit the door amongst a gang of other students. When he first seen her he couldn't believe it.

Queeny begin walking pass his car, and didn't even notice it. Phill raised down his window.

"Queeny get your ass in this car," Phill said.

She jumped right in the passenger seat.

"Girl where the fuck you been. I've been worried about you thinking something bad happen to you," Phill said. "I've been over my friends Susan house, me and your sister wasn't getting along. Your sister don't know how to treat people," Queeny said.

Phill wanted to curse her out, but he knew that it'll only make matters worst. Phill drove her around for hours talking to her on a civilized level. Telling her that she was a queen, and a beautiful human being, and that she deserve better than being some hoodrat or some low life drug addict.

Phill knew that the route she was going she was destine for self destruction.....

"Your momma and daddy's demise came from them running the streets and using drugs and I know you aint ready to die. And I aint ready to bury you in a casket. I love you as you're my very own. I always cared about you even when you was a little girl. I want for you the same things I'd want for my very own daughter if I had one," Phill said.

"I know in a few more years you're gonna be grown and you'll have to make your own decisions, but I hope that I can inspire you to be a great woman instead of a nobody. You're destine to be a queen in your own mind within time," Phill said.....

She ended up moving back into Rochelle's home, she stop selling dope and getting into trouble for the time being. Although she continued to smoke weed, she stayed away from the streets.....

CHAPTER 10

Q ueeny stayed out of trouble for a couple of years. Phill would spend lots of time with Queeny because he loved her and wanted her to be a success story of being an honest working citizen, and a respected business woman.....

By the time Queeny was sixteen Phill's Prince Black was checking her out, but Black knew if he got involved with her Phill would be pissed off. Prince was a snake in the flesh of a human, a dopefiend, killer, slash stick up man. King Phill made him the prince for one main reason; Phill knew that Black would run the ViceLord mob with an iron fist, and wouldn't take any bullshit.

Black even start hanging out with Queeny. Phill didn't mind, he figured Queeny was like Black's God daughter, or younger sister. Although Phill knew Black was a snake, but he didn't think he'd ever snake him.

When Black, and Queeny would hang out together they'd smoke weed and do average shit, like go to the show, shopping, or just riding around bending blocks.....

Around this point and time Queeny's grades begin to excel. She begin to get a higher learning with plans on being a college student......

~~~~~~~~~~~

Around the time Queeny was seventeen she was riding in the car with Phill. Phill was going to pick up some money that a nigga owed him. He usually had someone to take care of his drug business. The reason why he went this time to take care of this transaction himself was because he was only collecting money.

The reason he took Queeny with him was because she was already in the car.

Phill had been sweating this nigga to pay him some money he owed him. He'd fronted him Four and a half ounces of raw cocaine. But the nigga who owed him had been bullshiting on paying him; the nigga finally beeped him, and Phill called him as they made arrangements for Phill to come pick up the money he owed him.

Once Phill made it to his destination he parked in front of the building the nigga gave him the address to.

As soon as he finished parking the nigga that owed Phill the money ran up to the car in a mad man rage shooting, hitting Phill in the head three times......

At first the trigger man was unaware that Queeny was in the car until he start shooting up Phill. Once he shot Phill in the head the third time Queeny frantically tried to open the door, and get out of the car but didn't make it out; the trigger man shot her twice in the neck as she fell out the door on to the ground he then shot her once in the back, and fled the scene of the crime. In the back of his mind he was positive that he had killed Phill, and Queeny......

Silky Mac was the killer. Silky mac was one of Phill's long term homies. Phill had knew Silky Mac almost all his life and would've never thought he'd cross him especially not for something small as a four and a half.

Silky mac begin using more cocaine than selling, and ended up fucking up Phill's money. Usually when Silky Mac would pay Phill he'd be short. This time Silky Mac had fucked up more than half of the money. Silky Mac knew that if he didn't pay Phill, Phill would have his joint robbed repeatidly, or possibly have him shot or killed. Silky Mac had clout for the ViceLords, but not like Phill.

Silky mac figured that if he killed Phill and no one knew about it he would get away with the murder, paying Phill, and he wouldn't have to worry about no one doing anything to him.....

Phill had so many people attending the the funeral it was as if a celebrity had died. Silky Mac was one of the pallbearers.

After Phill got killed Phill's followers, and Silky Mac, and his guys walked the streets like Zombies; day and night, night and day trying to find out any information on who killed Phill.

I'f they'd ever found out who killed Phill, that individual or anyone else that was related or even affiliated with him would have to die.

Unfortunately the only witness was Queeny whom was in critical condition.....

Silky Mac had heard that Queeny survived. Silky Mac was only a little worried, although he assumed she didn't know him. He also figured that it happen so quick that she wouldn't recognize it was him, even if she did see him again.

Several days after the funeral everyone was still sad..... Although Phill was a gang cheif he did alot of good things for people: Paid peoples way through college, helped people with bills, even stopped people from getting killed or being endangered by his own ViceLord members. He even forced some people to rehab to stop their addiction. Phill had some bad ways, but he had some good ways as well.

For the next past couple weeks Phill's followers amongst others including homicide had been visiting Queeny daily anxious to know who was the killer, but she was still in critical condition.

By a twisted faith of luck this particular day and time Prince Black came to the hospital shortly after her recovery. Black was the first one whom seen her after her recovery. This first thing came out of Black's mouth was "who did this to you, and Phill." "Silky Mac," Queeny said. "Silky Mac," Black said in disbelief, surprised.

"Which Silky Mac," Black asked? "Conservative Silky Mac," Queeny said. "You sure it was Silky Mac," Black asked in disbelief?

As Queeny attempted to tell him she was sure it was Silky Mac Black mentally blocked Queeny out paused thinking to himself I only know one Silky Mac, and why would he kill Phill.

Queeny begin to vividly tell Black the horrifying story, as Black was focused listening attentively. As she talked it was as Black could visualize the ordeal as if he was actually there.....

"Phill had got a beep, looked at his beeper and told me to grab the celluar phone outta his glove department. He dial the number off his beeper. Once the person on the other line answered Phill asked him who is this. Then Phill was like Silky Mac what the fuck took you so long to get up with me. I don't know what Silky Mac said. Then Phill asked him did he have all the money he owed him. Phill then hung up and drove to where Silky Mac was.

We drove to this big brown building, and parked and then Silky Mac came outta nowhere shooting.

Black paused as his mind went blank for a few seconds, closed his eyes visualizing the bullets ripping through Phill's flesh putting him to death.

Black then opened his eyes.

"You sure it was Silky Mac, how do you know Silky Mac," Black asked? "I know it was Silky Mac because I heard Phill say

228

his name over the phone, and I know Silky Mac personally cuz he fucks with my friend Susan's mother," she said.

"Did you tell anybody about what happen," Black asked? "Naw I'm just waking up after I got shot," Queeny said. "Don't tell nobody, you hear me girl, don't tell nobody," Black said. "A'ight," Queeny said.

Black immediately left the hospital filled with rage. Once he entered his car he remembered that he had pictures of Silky Mac from the past that they took at a club.....

He went and got the pictures and went right back to the hospital.....

Once he made it back to the hospital he noticed that Rochelle, and her daughters were there. Black sat down and chilled out impatiently awaiting on Rochelle and her daughters to leave in order to show Queeny the pictures to see if she could positively I.D. Silky Mac.

Once Rochelle and her daughter's left Black showed her the pictures and told her to pick out which individual was Silky Mac. Each picture displayed a group of niggas on it. Black had already had it on his mind that if she could pick out Silky Mac outta the groups, then she was right in knowing who exactly took Phill's life from him.

With no hesitation she picked out Silky Mac on each and every picture..... "You bet not tell nobody about Silky Mac killing Phill, I'f they ask who killed Phill, and shot you tell them you don't know cuz it happen so fast," Black told her. "I know how this shit go, he took Phill's life know you'll take his, eye for an eye," Queeny said.

Black slightly smiled thinking to himself this girl gotta a little game under her belt.

"I gotta go, I gotta run some errands," Black said.

As Black sat in his car outside the hospital he tried to put all the puzzle pieces together. He remembered what Quenny said that he owed Phill some money.

But Phill a good nigga he would've gave him some work, or fronted him some shit to get on. Aw this nigga must've been fucking up the money and couldn't pay Phill back. So he told Phill to meet him outside the hood to collect, and once Phill came to collect he'd kill him, not knowing that Queeny would be with him. This pussy ass nigga came to the funeral, was even one of the pallbearers, and roamed the streets with us looking for the one that killed Phill, and all along he was the one who did it. He did all this shit so he wouldn't be suspect as the killer, Black thought to himself.

Black yelled out, "Bitch ass nigga."

At first Silky Mac wasn't hiding out because he assumed Queeny didn't see him when the shooting occured, and if she did see him during the shooting, she didn't know who he was. But now Silky Mac was hiding out he started to get nervous about if Queeny would recognize him or not.

What Silky Mac didn't know was Queeny already knew exactly who he was.....

Silky Mac was the chief of the Conservative ViceLords, which was a branch of Vicelords that didn't have a large number of members.....

Black told all the I.V.L. to kill any C.V.L. they see, and that anyone whom killed Silky Mac will be granted 50,000. Once people heard about that 50,000 everybody and their momma was looking for Silky mac. Most people didn't give a fuck about avenging Phill's death they were only interested in that 50,000.....

Less then an hour later it was casualties of street wars. The Insanes went everywhere the C's hung out at and caused blood shed. What made this war different was that the C.V.L's didn't know they was in war at first. Therefore they'd be somewhere chilling seeing members of the Insanes walk up, the C's would assume that they were just coming to kick it, or buy some drugs, all along they was coming to commit bloody murder.....

The streets was filled with madness, their was no peace or sleep, nothing but continuous gun-fire, death and destruction. It was like something out of a religious book. How the creator brought certain villages and towns to an end. Even the police was nervous to patrol the streets.....

The next day after Black gave word to the I.V.L. to slay Silky Mac or any other C.V.L. they'd came across, the C.V.L.'s begin to retaliate. The C.V.L.'s still didn't know what the war was about; the only thing they knew was that the Insanes was coming through fucking them up and that they must battle. The C's didn't stand a chance. The Insanes were deeper and had more heartless killers.....

Usually when two different branches of ViceLord had a problem they'd resolve it by putting someone in violation. It was rare that it resulted in gun-fire, and when it did it didn't last long, the chieves would squash the problem. But this war would be a never ending shed of blood because a king was killed. Never in the history of ViceLord existence was a king killed; usually the worst that would happen to a king was he'd get lots of time in the state or federal prison or die of a disease or even natural causes.

At this point in time, Silky Mac had went to a family reunion a day before the war kicked off.....

A day after the war he called one of his homies house in Chicago for nothing more than to tell him that the family reunion in Memphis was fun. When he called his homies Tim's house, before he could get a chance to explain how good the reunion was Tim begin snapping out.

"Lord we waring with the Insanes, it's like Vietnam in the streets. I aint never heard this much gun fire," Tim said. "What ya'll waring with the Insanes for," Silky Mac asked?

"I don't know man they just been coming through shooting motherfuckers, in broad daylight as if they don't even give a fuck.

"Make sure all the brother's are secure with guns and shit, I'll investigate to see what the problem is," Silky Mac said.....

Silky Mac called one of his ho's from the hood, and asked her why was it war in the streets amongst the C's, and the Insanes. He knew she'd know cuz she was the hoods spy detective, she stayed in everybody's business. Coincidently she knew what the war was about cuz her little brother was an Insane.

"They waring cuz they think you is the one that killed Phill," she said. "I aint kill Phill," Silky Mac said. "That's what they think, Black told the Insanes to kill any C.V.L. they see on site, and he got a price on your head for fifty g's," she said. "Why would they think I killed Phill, I got love for Phill, Phill was my guy," Silky Mac said. "I don't know, but I know that they think you was the one that killed Phill," she said.

Silky Mac immediately hung up the phone without even saying bye.

Silky Mac sat for hours trying to figure out who told Black that, because no one was around to witness the murder. Silky Mac knew that he was in for a world of trouble and figured that he'd better stay properly placed away from Chicago, in Memphis.

Weeks passed along and Silky Mac was still nowhere to be found.....

Now not only was Black and the Insanes looking for him, now homicide was to. Come to find out an old lady and her grandaughter had witnessed the entire murder, and attempt murder of Phill, and Queeny. At first they didn't wanna tell anyone because they was to scared that Silky Mac would kill them if he'd found out they'd told the police on him. But both the mother and grandaughter conscious got the best of them feeling guilty and decided to inform the authorities on what they'd witness. After homicide found out Silky Mac was the killer they went out on an all out man hunt.

Homicide begin repeatidly questioning Queeny about was Silky Mac the one whom killed Phill, and shot her. They'd continue to show her mugshots and other photos of Silky Mac. She continue to tell them that she didn't actually see who shot her..... Homicide could get a conviction with just the old lady, and her grandaughter as witnesses. But they knew that with Queeny, the old lady, and her grandaughter as witnesses Silky Mac would get found guilty beyond a reasonable doubt.

Queeny still never told no one but Black that Silky Mac was the one who did it. Black didn't want Silky Mac to go to prison. Black wanted to take his life as he'd took Phill's life. Black believed in the old school ritual that under no circumstances are you to work with the police. Other people believed that if you testify on someone as far as witnessing to family member or friend being shot then you wasn't actually snitching, because they shot a love one. But in reality if an individual works with the police an any shape, form, or fashion you're still a stool pigeon.....

Through it all Queeny told no one of Silky Mac being the one. The only reason that people in the streets knew that Silky Mac was the one who killed Phill was because Black told everybody. Black never told anybody that Queeny told him that. The only reason Black told people was so that they'd revenge Phill's death. Black couldn't just tell people to shoot up the C's without telling them that Silky Mac killed Phill.

Approximately one month after Black gave word to have all the C's and Silky Mac wacked, Silky Mac was still no where to be found. The C.V.L.'s on the other hand was either dead, killed by the Insanes. And those C's that wasn't killed got fucked up so bad that they wish they were dead. For the C.V.L's that were still alive they were hiding out; some even relocated to other states. During this war many Insanes, and some C's caught cases of violence, such as murders, attempt murders, arsons, gun cases, amongst other shit.....

One day Queeny asked Black, "Did you find Silky Mac yet." That was her indirect way of asking Black did he kill Silky Mac bitch ass yet. She knew that if Black ever caught Silky Mac he'd be in the history books. Black told her, "no I can't seem to find him." "Did you check on there spot out south," Queeny said?

Black paused looking at Queeny clueless.

"What spot out south," Black asked? "The C's got a block out south," Queeny said.

Black looked at Queeny angry as if he'd wanted to bite her head off.

"Why didn't you been tell me about this block out south," Black said. "I assumed you'd find Silky on your own," she said. "Where is this spot out south, and how do you know about it," Black asked? "It's around 73rd and Green," she said. "Aint no ViceLords around there that's all G.D's and B.D's," Black said. "The C's got one block around there. I know about this block, years ago Phill sont me to live with his sister out south for a little while; when I use to walk to the store I remember seeing Silky Mac standing on Green," she said. "How do know if it's one of the C's block, he could've knew some people around there and was rotaing with them," Black said. "Because I could tell, because everybody had their hats to the left. And Silky use to be standing around dictating things.".....

Black immediately left from Queeny on his destination to 73rd and Green. Black went by hisself in an unmarked car.

All the while driving over there he assumed that Queeny didn't know what she was talking about, because that area was filled with G.D's and B.D's that hated ViceLords.....

Once he finally made it to 73rd and Green he noticed that all the nigga's on that block wore there hats to the left. Then he noticed two of Silky Macs's guys that was from out west on the block, as well.....

Damn Queeny knew what she was talking about, Black thought to himself.

As he drove back to the hood he wondered how did they get a block in the heart of the G.D.'s. He then figured it out he'd seen Silky Mac at a club one time with some guys that had their hats to the right. Black could tell that the nigga's was baller's as far as getting money from the way they dressed; Silky Mac walked over to Black introduced his cousins to him. Black shoke their hands and they went their seperate ways.

Black figured out that Silky Mac family was G.D's whom had juice for the G.D's and let Silky get a block in their hood.

Later on that night Black and eleven of his guys went through 73rd and Green with fully loaded semi-automatic weapons. Killed ten men, and wounded seven others. This incident had the Chicago Police Department leery; because they'd never seen that amount of casualties and injuries all at once in over forty years within Chicago since Al Capone's St. Valentines Day Massacre. After that day the C.V.L.'s on 73rd and Green was no more. Those that wasn't out there to witness the mass blood shed was glad and decided to do other things with their lives after all the killings and imprisonments of other C.V.L.'s throughout the city in this short period of time. Some even flipped to join other gangs. Others left the street life alone, some even became Christians.....

Approximately six months later homicide found Silky Mac in Memphis, Tenessee over a family members house. He was brought back to Chicago's Cook County Jail, eventually convicted of the murder of Phill, and attempt murder of Queeny. Sentenced to fifty five years in prison.

Queeny never testified against him in court but the other two witnesses did. Silky Mac didn't last long in prison he was stabbed to death by some of King Phill's loyal followers..... Til this very day you'll never see to many C.V.L.'s in the streets of Chicago, or in Illinois prison system due to Silky Mac rat play and Slaying of King Phill.....

Printed in the United States
By Bookmasters